P9-AOZ-154

ℋℐ

75

THE SURROGATE GUN

Jack Cummings

Walker and Company
New York

Also by the Author

THE ROUGH RIDER
ONCE A LEGEND
REBELS WEST!
TIGER BUTTE
LYNCH'S REVENGE
SERGEANT GRINGO
DEAD MAN'S MEDAL

First published in the United States of America in 1990
by Walker Publishing Company, Inc.

Published simultaneously in Canada by Thomas Allen & Son
Canada, Limited, Markham, Ontario

Library of Congress Cataloging-in-Publication Data

Cummings, Jack, 1925–
The Surrogate Gun / Jack Cummings.
"Published simultaneously in Canada by Thomas Allen & Son, Canada,
Limited, Markham, Ontario"—T.p. verso.
ISBN 0-8027-4102-9
I. Title.
PS3553.U444S8   1990   813'.54—dc20   89-25005

Printed in the United States of America

2 4 6 8 10 9 7 5 3 1

CHAPTER 1

HOLT looked out through the window grime of the newspaper office again. He knew Canton would be coming.

Nobody had to tell him that.

On the counter in front of him was a stack of last week's edition of the *Rosario Record*. He was the editor, Bret Holt. And in the editorial column, under his byline, was his tirade against Rufe Canton.

Holt knew now he had been a fool to have written what he did. But some things a man just had to do, if he was going to go on calling himself a man. Besides, nobody had ever yet called him a coward. Not even during the two years he'd spent fighting in the War of the Rebellion.

When he came West, he was thirty years old, and had it in his mind to soak up the color of the country, and to get it down on paper. He was going to tell all those readers back East—avid readers, he hoped—how it really was out here on the frontier.

He hadn't figured then on the dust of Rosario's dirt main street soaking up his spilled blood. But that's how a man's plans can get sidetracked in five years.

He was so sure that Canton was coming that he'd got out his Shopkeeper's Model Colt from a desk drawer and cleaned and oiled it. He was wearing it now in a shoulder holster.

He knew how to use it. He'd learned during the late past, when he'd taken sides in the Lincoln County War. Taken sides editorially, that is; he hadn't been an active participant in the fighting.

Still, a frontier editor who takes sides in his territory's disputes can make himself vulnerable to great harm, and

1

he'd bought the gun and practiced with it until he could hit what he was shooting at.

So, if Rufe Canton was coming, he felt he was as ready for him as he would ever be.

To tell the truth, the adrenalin had him high enough that he was looking forward to the encounter. It made him wonder if other editors, whose pens and presses had led them into duels, had shared this feeling.

Such showdowns weren't a rarity in the West. But more often than not, they took place between peers, editors of rival papers who got to name calling. Or between editors and local politicians, neither usually adept with six-guns.

Rufe Canton was different. Hired gun was his usual business. That is, when he wasn't out of a job and went to robbing stage coaches, which was what Holt had just accused him of doing in his column.

Holt had been on the stage-run back from Socorro during its latest holdup, and he'd recognized Canton by his voice and manner despite the neckerchief over his face.

Canton had taken fifty dollars from Holt's own wallet, and the editor had given vent to his ire by calling him out in the *Record* as the bandit.

It wasn't likely that being accused of the crime bothered Canton much. He had long been suspected of outlawry, but never charged, and he had this little New Mexico town pretty well buffaloed by his swagger and his reputation. There was no lawman in Rosario; the nearest one was the sheriff, way over in Lincoln. And Canton had been getting along as he damned well pleased ever since the County War was over.

What would bother him was that Holt had made a call on his pride by daring to name him. And Canton couldn't allow that to pass without some kind of rebuttal.

And this was the day he was in town. This was the day he was coming. A pair of excited townsmen had stopped by earlier to warn Holt that Canton had just announced as much in McCleod's place where he had been drinking.

Holt's hired girl, Gloria, who had been setting type back in the shop, happened to come to the front just at that time and she overheard them. She stood just beyond the inner doorway until they'd left to go back to the saloon.

She stepped forward then, looking scared, and said, "What will you do, Bret? Oh, God, what can you do?"

She was a firm-bodied, slender young woman, with an attractive face, but a usually cool manner. The agitation in her voice now surprised him.

"I'll face him, Gloria. I'll not hide from him."

"You're a fool then," she said. "Get out of town. Run."

That's the way she was. Bold for a woman, when she spoke.

He thought her manner came from her being on her own for most of her life. She had survived in the West on a variety of jobs, some of which she mentioned when she applied for work with him: She had been a cook, waitress, dress shop-keeper, one-room school teacher, and printer's helper.

When she came to Holt, a few months before, she'd just arrived in Rosario, and had rented a shack at the end of the street. In those days, a single woman doing that was certain to arouse curiosity, even some sly innuendoes.

The people of the town soon learned not to voice these in Holt's presence. Not after he'd known her a few days and already his heart started jumping whenever he stood close to her.

She had dextrous fingers when it came to setting a case of type for his old Washington Hand Press. Just watching her fingers move excited him strangely. Even her reserve tantalized him. He was never sure if she returned his interest.

Up to the day of the shooting, he still didn't know.

"Go home, Gloria," he said, after she called him a fool. "Whatever happens, this is no place for you to be."

She stared at him, long and hard, and in her eyes he read something he did not understand. "You men and your fool pride."

She turned then and went back into the shop and cleaned

the ink from her fingers, and left from the rear door, not saying another word.

He went back to watching the street.

The sun was bright outside, and when he first saw the dark figure coming and caught the glint on the low-holstered gun, he was sure the time had come.

But as the figure came closer, he saw he was mistaken.

It wasn't Canton, it was Will Savage.

What fooled Holt at first was the way he swaggered. At some time or other, he thought, Will must have seen the way Canton walked. And he had a gift for mimicry, that was sure.

Watching him now, Holt shook his head.

To paraphrase an old song he'd heard somewhere, *I made him what he is today.* Before Holt, Will had been just another saddlebum who drifted into town one day, and ended up doing odd jobs wherever he could get them.

People liked him. He was a tall, strong, ruggedly handsome figure of a man in his late twenties. The kind of man who looked like he ought to be able to do better than he apparently ever had. He looked as if he was smarter than he was, too, as anyone discovered talking to him a while.

For all of that, he seemed content enough to just do what he was doing. Ambition and high hopes, it appeared, were things that didn't bother him.

It was only recently that he'd adopted the swagger. Or taken to wearing a gun either.

Holt knew this was all his fault. And all because, unlike Will, he had ambition. Holt's ambition went beyond being just a small town newspaper editor and job printer.

He had once dreamed of being a big Eastern daily journalist, and he'd come West hoping to send back dispatches that might land him a job as stringer for one of them, as a way to get started.

It hadn't worked out that way.

And then he began to read those Western dime novels such as were published by *Beadle & Adams* of New York, and he decided to write one himself. By that time he'd been in the West three years, and had absorbed a feel of it that showed through in his writing.

The novel sold.

His second one didn't.

One night he was sitting at a table in McCleod's place, commiserating with a passing whiskey drummer named Brady, who was buying, and to whom he related his disappointment with his literary career.

The drummer was an affable man, as a good salesman ought to be, and he said, "I've seen a lot of those dime novels scattered around the territory as I travel. And it seems to me the ones most popular have one thing in common. An author has got to get himself a series character. You know what I mean?"

"I think so."

"Look at what old Ned Buntline has done with Buffalo Bill Cody," he said. "Get yourself a real frontiersman for a hero."

"Where?" Holt said. "Hell, they've all been taken."

Right then, Brady pointed across the saloon at the swamper pushing along a broom. "There's *your* man," he said, and laughed. "Looks the part, don't he?"

"You mean Will Savage?" Holt said. "You're joking!"

"Will *Savage?*" he said. "Great name for a frontier hero."

Holt was silent.

"Yes, sir," Brady said. "Take away that broom, put him on a horse with a '73 Winchester and—I notice he's wearing range garb already."

"Only clothes he's got," Holt said. "Grubline rider, down on his luck temporarily."

"With his looks and name," Brady said, "and your imagination, you could make him into a series hero."

"I couldn't make him believable."

"Sure you could. Get him to pose for a photographer. Write a novel about him, and send the picture along with it to your publisher."

Well, maybe it was the whiskey, or maybe he touched a nerve, but what he said struck a chord in Holt.

When Brady came back through many months later, Holt told him he'd followed his suggestion. He was even able to hand him a newly printed copy of *Will Savage, Man of the West,* which *Beadle & Adams* had published with enthusiasm.

Brady skimmed through the pages, and said, "It must have been the photograph that did it." Then as he saw Holt's scowl, he laughed. "No. Damned good writing, Holt. Considering the genre." He paused. "Did he give up his job as swamper?"

"He sure did. As soon as he read the book."

"You giving him money to live on?"

"Hell, there're people all over town offering him small jobs. They like to have a celebrity working for them."

"Seems like you ought to give him something."

"I have," Holt said. "Enough for a brand new Peacemaker, and cartridges to practice shooting it."

"Sounds like he's taking himself seriously."

Holt nodded. "So much so, it worries me."

"It shouldn't. The more he plays the part, the more real your stories will appear to your readers."

Holt shook his head. "I don't like to see a poor bastard like him deluding himself." He paused, then said, "The hell of it is, folks around here are getting a kick out of helping him do just that."

"Let him have his fun," Brady said. "Lord knows, he's not likely had much of it thus far in his life."

"Maybe so," Holt said. "But I still don't like it."

Now, as Holt waited in the front of his printery for Canton, Will came in, and there was a worried look on his handsome face.

"Geez, Mr. Holt," he said, "I just found out Rufe Canton is gunning for you!"

Holt had to smile. There was something almost ludicrous

in the formal way Will always addressed him, even though
Will had become a national celebrity of sorts. Probably, Holt
thought, Will stood in awe of all those daring, imaginary
exploits Holt had concocted for him.

Will was a simple and honest man, and such lying must
have seemed to him a God-given accomplishment.

"I know," Holt said.

"Ain't you scared?"

"Some, maybe."

"I wish I'd had more practice shooting," he said.

"Why is that, Will?"

"Hell," he said, "don't you know? So's I could help you
better against Rufe when he comes."

"You keep out of this, Will," Holt said. "This is just between
him and me."

"You done me a big favor, Mr. Holt. Making me famous
and all. I owe you for that."

"I fight my own battles, Will," Holt said.

"You think you can take him?"

"I'm hoping," Holt said.

"You're a brave man," Will said. "You surely are. Geez!
Rufe Canton!"

"You'd best get out of here, Will."

"I got now so's I can hit a tin can two times out of five,"
Will said.

"I don't think that'd be good enough, Will."

Will thought about it, then said, "I reckon not. But I owe
you a try."

"You don't owe me, Will," Holt said.

"Well, I think I do. I wasn't nothing till you made me
somebody in that book you wrote."

"I made money on the book," Holt said. "That squares
us."

"You going to write another? About me?"

"I have it in mind, Will. All depends on what happens
when Rufe comes down that street."

"Hell, if you get killed, you won't be able to write it."

"You can't put it much plainer than that," Holt said. "Still, I don't want you here when he comes. I don't want you getting killed on my account. Whatever happens, I brought it on myself, and I'll face up to it."

Will frowned, as if trying to remember something, then he said, "If I recollect correct, I said them same words in the book."

"If I recollect, you did."

"Kind of makes us two of a kind then, don't it?" Will said. "And like kind ought to stick together."

Holt was getting exasperated with him. He said, "Will, you get the hell out of here and go back up the street and wait with the rest of the crowd. I don't want your blood on my hands."

Will gave him a long studying look, and Holt saw the understanding come into his eyes, and knew he'd got through to him his feelings.

Will turned to the door and went out, and Holt could see him heading for McCleod's, but now he was no longer swaggering.

Then, when Will was about fifty yards from the saloon, Canton stepped out from under a portico and down into the street, and started walking toward the newspaper office.

Will saw him and stopped in his tracks as if he was frozen. His back was to Holt so Holt couldn't see his face, but could see the hard look on Canton's.

When they were about ten yards apart, Canton stopped and called out some words that Holt couldn't distinguish. Then he stood there, not moving either, his legs planted a little apart, and his slash of a mouth baring his teeth in a grin.

They stood that way for one of the longest minutes Holt ever endured. Poor dumb son of a bitch! Holt thought. Don't do it, Will, don't for chrissakes do it!

Will shook his head then and began to walk again, and

Canton threw back his head and laughed, and in a moment they were passing each other.

Now Canton was coming toward Holt, and he was no longer laughing. He had business on his mind, and he was out to get it over.

Holt reached under his arm and gripped the butt of his Shopkeeper's, and realized then that his palm was slick with sweat. He withdrew his hand and wiped it across the leg of his pants.

Holt moved to the door, knowing it was time to step out, but finding it was hard to do. He had his left hand on the knob, but hesitated, watching Canton's approach through the glass panel.

Canton was only a few doors away now, and had just come abreast of Gold's Dry Goods when Gloria suddenly ran out toward him and clutched at his sleeve in what must have been a vain hope to dissuade him.

Canton stopped, but only for a moment. He turned his head and looked at her, then reached out and grabbed the high collar of her clothing and ripped it out down to her waist, so that her full breasts thrust out against her frilly undergarments to be stared at by half the men of the town who were watching.

Canton grinned then, faced Holt's way again, and resumed walking.

In her shocked embarrassment she grabbed up her ripped dress, trying to hide her semi-nakedness, and retreated.

Holt stepped out onto the street.

He stepped out shooting. No gentleman editor's *code duello* now. No damned dime-novel foolishness about who could make a fastest draw. He was mad clear through at what Canton had done to Gloria.

So mad that he missed him, even though he got off the first two angry shots.

What happened next was only what he felt and heard as he lay in the street in a state of shock.

He could hear Canton's gun firing and feel the bullets as they poured into him, with a spaced sequence.

Right shoulder, left arm, left leg, right leg.

Canton had a bullet left, if he'd chambered five, which was the custom.

The fifth didn't come.

Instead, Holt heard his words. Or thought he did, although it might have been days later that he heard them from Gloria, who had been close enough to hear him call them.

Rufe said, "I won't kill you now, Holt. I'll get my kicks by watching you suffer now—and heal up, if you can. I hope you do. I'm leaving for a range war up Colfax County way. But I'll come back. And when I do, we can do this again. You think about that while I'm gone."

Holt heard him laugh then, last thing before he passed out.

Thinking about this later, it all sounded crazy. Then Holt remembered that a lot of gunfighters roaming around the West were nothing more than psychopathic killers.

He was a long time healing, and it was Gloria, of course, who nursed him. She and old Doc Sanderson saved him.

Old Doc had come to Rosario a year before and lived the life of a recluse until somebody passing through recognized him from down El Paso way, and let out that he was a doctor.

He was perhaps the oldest person in town, and after he was exposed, he kept saying that he was retired from medicine. Still, he never could refuse to treat anyone who seriously needed it.

His hands were pretty shaky, but he still managed to extract two bullets from Holt, including the one in his shoulder. The other two had gone clear through.

He had an old man's bluntness, and when Holt came around enough to speak and asked him if he was going to live, Doc said, in that high, quavering voice of his, "You think you should, you damned fool?"

That made Holt mad enough to say, "I sure as hell do!"

Doc snorted and said, "Well, maybe you will, then."

Holt figured he was a grumpy because he'd given Doc such a major job to do, considering his diminishing abilities. During the weeks Holt was recovering, Doc never came around to check on him unless Gloria went personally to bring him.

One of those times, he said, "Dammit! Holt, she's better for you than I am."

Anyhow, between the two of them, Holt was getting well.

He would have thought that as he got better, Gloria would have become more cheerful. But she didn't. It seemed that as he approached full recovery, she became more and more morose.

At first he just put this to her natural reserve, but later he saw it was something else. Finally, he asked her straight out what was troubling her, besides nursing him. By then he was up and around, although not yet spry by any means.

"It's *him*," she said.

"Doc?"

"Not Doc!" she said, angered. "Him, *him!* Rufe Canton!"

She gave him a scare when she said that, one like he'd never felt before. Holt knew then that all those wounds had changed him. "He's back?" he said.

"Not yet," she said. "But he will be."

"Maybe not."

"He will be," she said flatly.

"What makes you so sure?" he said. "He's still up there in Colfax County, isn't he?"

"There's a fight going on up there over land grants," she said. "The word is, he's hired out his gun to a big land and cattle company."

He felt a sliver of hope. "Maybe he'll get killed up there."

She shook her head, but didn't say anything.

He didn't believe it himself, so he didn't push the point. Not Canton, he thought. Sooner or later he'll be back. Holt knew it just as strongly as she did. He didn't know how he knew. He just did.

Then she asked, finally, the question he dreaded. "If he comes back," she said, "will you fight him again?"

"Will you?" she said.

He couldn't bring himself to say it, so he didn't answer. All those wounds had changed him, all right.

Canton had known they would. He'd get his kicks out of that just like he said he'd do.

He forced himself to meet her eyes, and he could see a disappointment there as she realized he had lost his nerve.

But hadn't she once told him to run? he thought.

She held him with her stare, and her words came tightly when she spoke again. "He deserves to die," she said. "Don't you remember what he did?"

"He shot hell out of me," he said.

"Not that," she said. "What he did to me."

He had to think back to remember, and she spoke just as he recalled it.

"Me," she said bitterly. "Me standing there shamed and half-naked in front of the whole town. He's got to be killed for that."

So even though she'd nursed him back to health from his wounds, it was as if she held him to fault for her disgrace.

It was a thing that came between them.

And they had been close to becoming lovers.

CHAPTER 2

THEY were a lost couple, he and Gloria, each with his own obsession.

His was the fear of Canton's return, hers was the craving for vengeance against Canton.

After Holt recovered, it seemed that nothing would ever bring them together again, although after he resumed publishing the *Record* she came back to work for him.

But if there had been her reserve standing as a block to his desires before, now there was a bitter coldness.

He wanted her more than ever, because he longed for the respect she'd had for him before he had lost it by his dread of being shot up again.

It was more than mere dread. It was terror. If others found that hard to believe in a man who once prided himself on courage, they should try having bullets fired deliberately into four different parts of their bodies, in the space of a few seconds.

He couldn't forget the terrible pain of it, but worse yet was his remembrance of Canton's words: "When I come back, I'll do this again."

Even so, it was Gloria who found something they had in common. That something was Will Savage.

As Holt had told the whiskey drummer, Brady, he had earlier presented Will with a Colt Peacemaker, and had paid for cartridges from Kelly's Hardware when he started building Will up as a frontier hero, just in case Beadle & Adams should send some representative out West to meet Holt's fearless protagonist.

Then, when he was laid up and unable to run the newspa-

13

per, he had cut Will off from his account as Kelly's. But every now and then, from a swale behind the falsefronts on the south end of town, he and Gloria would hear above the noise of the press the sound of shots being fired.

One day Gloria said, "About once a week somebody is out there firing away. I wonder who?"

That was about as close to intimate conversation that they had got since she found out he'd lost his nerve.

He looked up from a page he was proofreading. "Will Savage, maybe," he said.

Then, before he thought to stop her, she went out the rear door, presumably to investigate.

He was sorry right then that he had spoken. A woman had no business going out there where some fool, half-drunk maybe, could be blasting away wildly.

She was gone a long time, and when she came back there was a strangely thoughtful expression on her face.

"It's him," she said.

"Will?"

"Yes. And I had a talk with him." She paused. "Do you know he's spending what little he can spare from working odd jobs to buy ammunition for target practice?"

"I used to pay for it," he said.

"You ought to do it again."

"I don't see any real reason," he said, "now that he's come to living the role I've given him."

"The reason is," she said, "I never saw such shooting."

He nodded. "Yeah, he once told me he could only hit a tin can twice out of five."

"I mean," she said, "that he never misses now."

"What?"

"Not just tin cans," she said. "He never misses anything he shoots at. Tin cans, little stones lying on the ground. He even shot the head off a snake at fifty feet."

"Will did that?"

"That's why you ought to keep him practicing," she said,

coldly. "You might be able to hide behind his gun when Rufe Canton comes back."

That hurt, and Holt flared back. "There was a time I wouldn't take that from you."

"There was a time," she said, "when I wouldn't have said it."

She turned on her heel then and went back to work. He didn't follow her. He let the matter drop.

But he didn't forget it. Not the slur, of course, and not the suggestion either. He stopped by Kelly's later and told him it was all right to put Will's cartridge purchases on his account again.

Kelly gave him an oddly thoughtful look but didn't say anything, just nodded.

The next day Will stopped by to thank Holt.

"Glad to hear that your shooting is improving," Holt said.

"I been working hard at it," Will said. "Now that you give me a reputation to live up to."

"That's fine, Will."

Gloria left her typesetting and came over to them.

Will jerked off his hat and looked at her. "Ma'am," he said.

"I told Mr. Holt what an expert pistol shot you've gotten to be," she said.

"Yes, ma'am," he said. "I got now so's I can hit what I'm looking at, most every time. I reckon it's a knack comes natural to me."

"You and I ought to talk some more about it, one of these evenings," Gloria said. "I find it fascinating."

"Ain't much to it, ma'am, really," Will said. "Not for me anyhow, after I once't caught on. I just hold the gun and point the barrel of it like it was my finger, and squeeze. The gun, it does the rest."

"You're too modest, Mr. Savage," she said. "I'll just bet you could shoot rings around Mr. Holt here."

"No ma'am," he said. "I couldn't do that."

"Why not?"

"Because he's my friend."

"You wouldn't want to show him up, is that it?" She glanced at Holt.

"No, ma'am," Will said.

"You stop by my place some evening," Gloria said to Will, "and we'll talk about it."

"Talk about what, ma'am?"

"About how good you're getting with that gun."

"But you already seen that," he said. "Yesterday."

"You come by some evening, anyway. Tonight, if you like."

"Why thank you, ma'am. I might do that." He turned his head to look at Holt. "That's if'n Mr. Holt don't mind none."

"Mr. Holt doesn't own me." She met Holt's stare as she said it.

"He don't? I mean I thought—"

"You come by," she said. "You hear?"

"Yes, ma'am," he said. "I best be going now though. They got a busted door on the hotel outhouse, and they're going to pay me to fix it."

As soon as Will left, Holt said to her, "You shouldn't do that, you know."

"Do what?"

"Ask him to your place. People will talk."

"They already talk," she said, the bitterness coming back into her voice. "They will never stop talking about me standing naked in the street."

"It wasn't your doing," he said.

"Do you think that makes a difference? Women avoid me. The most I get from them is a smirking glance. Little boys point at me and giggle. And every man in Rosario looks at me as if I were fair game."

"They aren't thinking clearly about it," he said.

"Of course they're not! But you should know that's the way people are when they see a juicy bit of scandal to talk about."

She was right about that, and he couldn't think of anything to say.

Gloria went on. "And it isn't just here in Rosario that they tell about it, I'll wager. By now, the story of how Rufe Canton stripped me down is probably known over half the Territory, his reputation being what it is."

"I'm sorry," he said. "It should never have happened."

"If you had run from him, like I told you to do, it wouldn't have."

"I had my pride."

"Yes," she said, "you *had* it. And where is it now?"

"It seems to me," he said, "that your whole attitude toward backing down has changed."

"What happened to me can do that to a woman," she said.

He couldn't deny that. She was living proof that it was so.

What she said weighed heavily on him, because it lay between them, and he knew of no way to clear it up.

There was the other thing that bothered him greatly. It, too, was planted in his mind by her, and continued to grow. He kept hearing her words again and again when she'd said, coldly: "You might be able to hide behind his gun when Rufe Canton comes back."

He threw himself into work on another novel to send to Beadle & Adams, trying to lose his personal problems in a fictional world. But as he built up Will Savage's prowess on paper, he found himself more and more wanting to believe Will's invincibility was real.

He told himself, in clearer moments, that if he ever allowed Will to be tested in reality Will was certain to die as his surrogate.

Could a man be so driven by desperation that he'd risk a

friend's death on the outside chance it might save his own life?

He didn't like the answer he gave himself.

Still, Will *could* have a chance, he thought.

Such is what terror can do to a man.

CHAPTER 3

HOLT did not know what happened that night when Will went calling on Gloria at her shack in response to her insistent invitation. But he did know that whatever it was, it later caused Will to drop in whenever he was passing by the shop, just to have a few words with her.

Words that never told Holt anything, even though he made every effort to overhear them.

He only knew what he suspected. And that was enough to nearly drive him mad. There was a time when he might have let Will know his feelings, but now there were factors that held him back.

The biggest, and probably the only one really, was Will's growing stature in the eyes of the people of Rosario. Others, besides Gloria and himself, had witnessed his impressive marksmanship by spying on his target practice down in the wash at the edge of town.

Word spread, and the townsmen began to greet Will with new respect. Nobody now seemed to consider him a fool, as they once had when he'd first begun his posturing.

Holt realized now that what amounted to a transformation was taking place. And one great boost to it, that clinched it really, came when the native New Mexicans of the old-town part of Rosario threw their annual great celebration of *Cinco de Mayo*. The Fifth of May was the day in 1862 when the Mexicans defeated a French Army force at the battle of Puebla, in Mexico.

Old Town was a section of adobe dwellings that had been there before the first gringos ever came to Rosario. It adjoined, on the north, the wooden false-fronts of the Anglos,

19

and there was an easy commerce between sections that was peculiar to the Territory, and not always to be found in other parts of the Southwest.

Not even in California, and certainly not in Texas.

And, with the customary generosity of the Latinos, the Anglos were invited to participate in the celebration.

Although it was not the Mexican Independence Day, Cinco de Mayo could best be likened in color to the Anglo's Fourth of July, only with a flamboyant Hispanic flavor.

It was an attraction that annually brought most of the residents of clapboard gringo town to attend.

And most of whatever itinerants of either race who happened to be in the vicinity at the time.

One of these happened to be a Mexican *pistolero* from the province of Chihuahua, a suspected rustler and bandit, greatly feared among his own people on either side of the border.

His name was Chango Carmona, and he was said to have killed many men.

He was recognized soon enough by the crowd, who eyed him in awe, but he did not become rowdy until he had drunk heavily of *sotol*, which was vaguely like tequila and available at the fiesta.

Carmona dressed himself in the range clothes of a gringo, at least when north of the border. This was, possibly, in an effort to make himself less suspect to the gaze of any lawman on the lookout for him.

The clothes, though, could provide only a limited camouflage. He was a chunky and swarthy man, but his eyes were a rare blue.

They startled you when you first saw them, and when they were bloodshot from too much *sotol* as they were now, they startled you even more, with a kind of frightening madness that stared out.

Gloria and Holt were both there at the celebration, but not

together. She had chosen Will as her escort, and Will, obviously, was a willing choice.

They sighted one another as they watched one of several *mariachi* bands, and they exchanged nods, but remained apart.

Presently, with the shifting crowd, they strolled along a lane bordered on either side by open-front displays offering games of skill or chance for a few coins, such as have been part of fairs, Holt guessed, throughout history.

At the far end of the lane, so as not to offer danger to the strollers, some enterprising native had set up a small shooting gallery, back-stopped by a windowless adobe wall of his domicile.

He offered crude, homemade dolls as prizes for marksmanship. For weapons, he provided a choice of a pair of small caliber pistols.

And as Gloria and Will reached the end of the promenade, it was only natural that she would call Will's attention to this concession.

From where Holt stood, a few yards away, he could see Will smile as she led him toward it.

Will exchanged a few words with the man in charge, then accepted the light-calibered weapon the native handed him.

He sighted in on the targets, one by one, firing fast until he emptied the chambers.

He had no misses.

That's what it took to win a prize. The native looked surprised, but selected a doll that Gloria pointed to, and presented it to her with a flourish. His white teeth flashed in a smile. It appeared he appreciated good shooting.

Will turned to leave, but he had taken only a couple of steps before Carmona, the blue-eyed gunslinger, was in front of him, barring his way.

Carmona was swaying from side to side. Holt could tell, even from where he stood, that Carmona was drunk.

Holt moved in toward them, wanting to hear what they were saying.

He heard Carmona say, "You shoot good, *hombre*. Somebody tell me there is a hombre got a name of Savage, is good with a gun. Maybe you been him, eh?"

Will smiled. "Yep, I got a book writ about me."

"A book? *Un libro*? You must be pretty good, eh?"

Will's smile became a grin. He pointed to the doll that Gloria was holding. "Good enough for that," he said.

"Ai-ee!" Carmona said. "You plenty good enough for doll, looks like. You good enough for man?"

Will's grin faded, and he frowned. "What do you mean?"

"I mean, how many men you kill?"

"Hell, I never killed no men, really," Will said, "only in the book that my friend, Mr. Holt, writ about me."

"I think you and me, we ought to have a contest."

Holt thought right then that it was time for Will to look scared, but he didn't.

"Sure," he said. "I reckon that would be fun." Then, without another word, he turned back to the improvised shooting gallery.

Carmona stared after him, looking stunned by Will's failure to understand. He gave a jerky shake of his head, as if to clear it, and followed Will to the booth.

The owner had a scared look as they approached. He stood there motionless, then went into a rush of words. "You want to shoot, señores? *Bueno!*" He took up one of his target pistols in either hand and held them out.

"Not them!" Carmona said. "Not them toys, hombre." He patted the heavy Colt .44 he wore high on his hip, Mexican style.

Abruptly then, he jerked it out of his holster and fired a shot into one of the paper targets fastened to the wood frame which leaned against the adobe wall.

The big caliber bullet blew the target apart as it slammed

into the wall behind, tearing out a huge pit and sending back flying chunks of adobe.

A fragment struck the vendor, and he cried out, "Please no, señor Carmona! Is my house behind there!"

For answer, Carmona emptied his gun at the remaining targets, filling the booth with debris and dust as his bullets ripped into the wall.

The vendor had thrown himself on the floor, and was no longer in sight. It was shooting enough to scare any man.

Any man except Will, apparently. He had a look of anger on his face. "You had not ought to've done that!" he said to Carmona.

Drunk as he was, Carmona laughed. He was still holding his gun. "So what you want to do about it, eh?"

Will had his own gun out now and he raised it to point at Carmona's chest. "Don't do that no more, you hear?" he said.

Carmona's laugh faded, and he lifted his weapon and you could hear the hammer being cocked, and then he pulled the trigger.

It seemed that everybody, including the drunken Carmona himself, had forgotten he'd used his shells on the targets.

Will, late, pulled his trigger too.

Holt stood there, transfixed by what had happened.

Carmona was on the ground, blood welling up and over-flowing from a hole in his chest. He jerked once, then was still.

A native, standing near, crossed himself.

The crowd which had been close enough to see it happen moved in, and somebody, a gringo, toed Carmona with his boot.

"He's dead," he said, wonder in his voice.

"Dead?" Will said.

"Dead," the man said. "Savage, you done killed Chango Carmona, for chrissakes!"

"Wasn't my intent," Will said.

There was an instant of silence after he said that, an instant and that was all, before Gloria's voice sounded, addressing him. "Keep your mouth shut, Will," she said sternly, almost under her breath. "You hear me?"

Will gave her a blank look. He didn't say anything, but it was plain that he'd heard, even if he didn't really understand.

But Holt did. Gloria had a plan, it was that simple.

And Holt kept his own mouth shut, too.

CHAPTER 4

WELL, Gloria knew what she was doing, Holt thought.

Before that afternoon was over, the word was out through the fiesta crowd, and the rest of the town of Rosario, and on its way, Holt guessed, across the whole Territory of New Mexico. Word that Will Savage had gunned down the Mexican badman, Chango Carmona.

Through one foolish misunderstanding and its freak consequence, Savage had gained a real reputation as formidable as the fictitious one Holt had concocted for him in his novels.

Within days, the native New Mexicans were referring to him as *El Salvaje*, The Savage. And, as such things go, he now stood bigger in their minds than had Carmona.

Of course, all along, during his recovery and after, Holt had harbored the inclination to run, to leave the Territory. But some trace of the pride he'd once had detained him. It kept him in Rosario just long enough until the possibilities that existed in Will took hold of his mind.

Word came that the expected range war up in Colfax County was still in the standoff stage. Sides had been taken, gunmen like Rufe Canton had been hired by either faction, and some sporadic shooting incidents had occurred. But the opposing forces seemed hesitant to bring the conflict to a head.

Holt's own thought, on hearing this, was that each feared to be the loser, and the loser would be far worse off than now. Such it was with wars.

But the time was near when each would have to take the chance.

He could relate to such feelings, because his own situation was, in its way, not unlike theirs.

A stranger came to Rosario.

Holt was staring out onto the street from the *Record* office and saw him riding in on a *grullo* gelding.

He wore a gambler's clothes that were a close match to the grullo's gray. A single-breasted frock coat, shirt, trousers, of the same shade. Only his black gun rig, boots, saddle and tack made a contrast. These, too, were a match for the horse, for its black muzzle, tail and lower legs.

The rider and mount together made a striking sight to see.

As Holt watched, he saw the rider turn to read his shop sign. He reined up for a moment, then rode the grullo toward it, dismounted and tied up at the hitchrack.

Holt was still seated behind his desk when the stranger came in.

"Bret Holt?" he said. There was no expression on his face.

Holt nodded, and got up to approach the counter. "You read it on the sign."

"I'd heard the name before."

"Glad the *Record* is a well-known newspaper," Holt said.

"Not the paper's name. Yours."

"Mine?"

"When Canton gunned you down, you made the front page down El Paso way."

"A hard way to gain fame," Holt said.

"I saw your name also on the cover of one of those dime dreadfuls, and put two and two together. You're the same Bret Holt?"

Holt nodded.

"I read the book."

"Glad to hear it."

"Pure, unadulterated horse crap," the stranger said. "All

about this character calls himself Will Savage. Even the name doesn't ring true."

"You've got to tell people what they want to hear," Holt said, "if you want to make money."

The other nodded. "I figured you'd made up this Savage character out of whole cloth." He paused. "Then word came that this Savage character had killed the Mex, Carmona." He gave Holt a hard stare. "Is that true?"

"It's true."

"That's harder to believe than your made-up stories."

"I think so myself."

The stranger thought that over for awhile. He was about Holt's age, but his clean-shaven faced had a gambler's pallor. Finally, he said, "My name is John Reno. Mean anything to you?"

Holt shook his head.

"It's better known over Arizona way," Reno said. "Gambler. Tucson, among other places."

"Known for what?" Holt said.

"Just known."

"Gambler gets known," Holt said, "it's mostly for gunplay."

"A time or two," Reno said. "But only if it was him or me. The gambling part is my business, the gun part isn't."

"Glad to hear that," Holt commented. "You said you read what happened to me?"

"Yeah, I guess. Holt, what's going to happen?"

"Happen where?"

"Here. When Rufe Canton comes back. That story I read in El Paso, it described his threat—about coming back and all."

"I'm sweating it out."

"I'd bet on that."

"Sure you would," Holt said. "You're a gambler."

"Exactly. And that's why I'm here."

Holt gave him a questioning look.

"Could be some sizeable bets placed when Canton comes back," Reno said.

"You must be joking. Who the hell wouldn't bet on Canton over me after what he did the last time?"

"Canton against you isn't what I had in mind."

"Who then?" Holt knew what he was getting at but he wanted to hear *him* say it. It wasn't something he'd yet allow himself to put into words.

Holt said, "What are you driving at?"

Reno gave him a long appraising stare before he spoke. "Are you so dense you can't see how it could be?" He paused, then shrugged and said, "This character, Will Savage—you made him famous."

"So?"

"Nobody ever heard of him until that book came out. So the way I see it, he owes you."

"Owes me what?"

"Gratitude, man, gratitude! I'd guess he'd be a friend of yours."

"More or less."

"Well, then. He must be one hell of a *pistolero* to take Carmona. And by now he's no doubt got pride in his ability. It shouldn't take much coaxing on your part to turn him into your protector."

"Maybe my mind doesn't run that way," Holt said. His words sounded too loud when he said it.

A grin cracked Reno's lips. "Is that right?" He paused. "Well, maybe not," he said. "But now I've put the bee in your bonnet, haven't I?"

Holt didn't answered him.

"Savage against Canton, now that's a match could draw some heavy betting," Reno said.

"You come all the way up from El Paso because of that?"

"Gambling is what I do. And a man like me, if he makes the right pick, can make a killing."

"A killing on a killing," Holt said bitterly.

"Exactly."

"You could lose, too."

"I figure on making the right pick."

"You know what you are?" Holt said. "You're a goddam ghoul."

"I've been called worse things in my day."

Their voices had been rising as they talked, and suddenly Gloria had come in from the shop and stood in the doorway. She stared at Reno as if she was seeing a ghost.

Reno stared back, looking as shocked.

"Johnny!" she said. Then, "I thought I recognized your voice."

His grin came back. "Been a while since you heard it," he said.

"A long while, Johnny."

"Cynical as ever, I see."

He said, "You must have known I couldn't stay put. Goes with my profession."

Holt did not like what he was hearing. It hinted at things unknown to him. And of things she hadn't named as work experience when she'd applied for a job with him.

"You two sound like old friends," he said. He tried not to let his concern show through.

Reno kept his eyes on hers. He said, without turning his head, "We once had the same employer. In Tucson."

Gloria's face flushed. "It wasn't exactly the way it sounds," she said to Holt.

Holt said, "All the gamblers I've know have worked in saloons and gambling houses."

"Our natural habitat," Reno said. He seemed to be enjoying this.

Gloria didn't. "I worked as a maid for his boss's wife," she said. "In their home."

"That's different," Holt said.

His words seemed to irritate her. "Is it?" she said. "Are you sure, Bret?"

"I'm sure," he said.

"Not all saloon girls are easy women," she said.

"So why do you labor the point?"

"A matter of principle. It's hard for a woman alone to survive," she said.

"I'll not argue that either."

Reno was noticing the ink on her fingers. He said, "This is a woman who will survive, no matter where she is."

"Yes," Holt said. "I believe that." He paused. "What I don't know is what there is between you."

"Bygones, Bret," Gloria said.

Reno's face hardened. "It takes two to make a bygone, Gloria."

She looked ready to make an angry reply. But suddenly her eyes dropped to the handle of his gun protruding from the drape of his frock coat.

She stared. Then she said, softly, "You may be right, Johnny. Are you staying in Rosario a while?"

"Maybe. I came on business."

"Perhaps I'll see you then."

"No perhaps about it," Reno said. "What we had, a man doesn't forget."

Then, as if Holt wasn't standing there, or perhaps because of it, she said, "Maybe a woman doesn't either, Johnny."

If she had in mind to stir Holt up, she succeeded. And if she wanted to stir up Reno, she did that too. Holt could tell by the way Reno's eyes fed on her figure as she turned and walked through the doorway and entered the shop.

"A lot of woman, Holt," Reno said. "A hell of a lot of woman."

"I don't like your mouth," Holt said.

Reno turned and stared. Then he said, "A man who's been shot to tell like you've been, he ought to speak more cautious, friend."

Looking into his cold eyes, Holt felt he was right. His brief surge of nerve failed him.

CHAPTER 5

A WEEK later a young cowboy, wearing a new-looking gun-belt and holster and six-gun, rode into Rosario on a strawberry roan.

Several people noticed his arrival, but paid him little mind. He wore working cowboy clothes, and this was cattle country. The just-bought look of his gun rig might have brought a smile had anyone noticed. It wasn't unusual for a young cowhand to ape the appearance of those fictional protagonists he'd read about in the *Beadle* novels or those of *Street & Smith*.

This had been a fact for long enough that it caused no particular attention any more.

The young rider tied his horse in front of McCleod's place and went in.

Jason McCleod was behind his bar. It was morning, and he was alone. He looked up at this, the first protential customer of the day, and nodded.

Something clicked in McCleod's mind. He'd seen this kid somewhere before. Well, maybe not. Maybe one just like him.

"Whiskey," the kid said.

He looked to be maybe eighteen, McCleod thought. "Sure," McCleod said. He placed a glass on the bar, reached below it for a bottle and poured the drink.

The kid tossed it off in one gulp.

McCleod kept staring at him, although he didn't know why. It wasn't something McCleod did very often. He'd long ago seen the elephant and heard the owl. But this kid seemed different.

The kid put down his empty glass. He didn't shove it out for a refill. His eyes raised to catch McCleod's stare.

"What the hell you looking at?" he said.

"You got a familiar look. Like I seen you somewhere before."

"How long ago?" the kid said.

"Maybe ten years back. I don't know."

"Hell, I was only eight years old then," the kid said.

"That's what bothers me," McCleod said.

"Up Cheyenne way, maybe?"

"That's it! Anybody ever tell you that you look like Gus Hatch?"

"Two-Gun Gus," the kid said. "He was once a big man up Wyoming way, I heard."

"Damn if you ain't a ringer for him when he was young," Jason said. "I didn't mean to stare, kid, but now you can understand why."

"You knew him?"

"He was killed in my place up there," McCleod said. "Killed when his quick draw struck the edge of a poker table. Only way it could have happened, my way of thinking."

"So I've heard."

McCleod was staring again, thinking back to that night in Cheyenne. "You related?"

"Two-Gun," the kid said, "he was my old man. So I been told."

"I'll be damned!" Jason said. "Small world, ain't it?" He paused, then said, "You talk like you never knew him."

"That's a fact. He took off, they tell me, right after I was born."

"You got a name, kid?"

"Not yet."

"Ain't what I meant," Jason said, a trace of irritation showing.

"Frank. Frank Hatch. From over Magdalena way."

"Well, Frank, I hope you don't take after your pa."

"I been thinking on it."

"Don't."

"I been hearing about this Will Savage here."

"I seen your old man die. I don't want to see it happen to you. Savage killed Carmona, kid."

"I ain't no Mex," the kid said.

"You're no Carmona, neither," Jason said.

"How do you know?"

"Hell, you haven't wore that gunbelt long enough to get it sweat stained."

"I wore out the one I had," the kid said, after a minute.

"Doing what?"

The kid was fiddling with his glass on the bar top with his left hand. Jason's eyes were on the kid's gun rig as he spoke, but even so, he didn't see what happened.

The gun was holstered, and then it was in the kid's right hand, pointing at Jason's belly. "Practicing this," he said.

Jason had a pale, indoor face, but now it was even paler. "Maybe I been mistaken," he said.

"Maybe you have," Frank Hatch said. He slipped his gun back into its sheath.

"You got a fast draw, all right. But it's not enough, kid. You got to hit at what you're looking." Jason was still a little shaken by what he'd seen.

"Come again?" the kid said.

"I mean, you got to hit what you're looking at."

"I can do that too," The kid looked around, saw the big clock on the wall. "See that clock pendulum swinging back and forth?"

"Hold it!" Jason said. "I believe you, Frank."

"You sure? I just as soon show you."

"I'm sure. A clock like that don't come cheap."

The kid nodded.

"There's ain't any future in a gunhand's life, Frank."

"Damn sight less in punching cows."

Jason couldn't think of any way to argue that. Once, a long time ago, he'd tried cowboying himself.

The batwing doors opened and the newcomer, Johnny Reno, came in.

Frank Hatch's interest was instant. "That Will Savage?" he said in a low voice.

"Hell, no, kid," Jason said. "Will ain't much older than you." He paused, then said, low too, "Johnny Reno. Gambler."

"Gambler, eh?" Frank Hatch said.

Reno came over to them, his eyes dropping to the stiff new gun rig the kid was wearing. He started to speak, but flicked his glance up to Jason's face as he did. He saw the quick warning there, and closed his mouth. He turned back to the kid and gave him a studying look.

"What're *you* looking at?" the kid said.

"Nothing," Reno said. "Nothing at all."

"What do you mean, nothing?"

"I didn't mean to stare."

The kid's glance dropped to the gun bulging just inside Reno's frock coat. "That's different," he said.

"Reno," Jason said, "meet Frank Hatch. Old Two-gun Gus's boy."

Reno's face showed interest. "Gus Hatch's son?"

"That's him," Jason said.

"I suppose *you* met my old man, too," the kid said, with some sarcasm.

"Never did," Reno said, "But I heard plenty about him."

"Good or bad?"

Reno was sizing him up, weighing his answer to that. He was a gambler, and he made his choice. "Good," he said.

"Frank was asking about Will Savage," Jason said.

"That a fact?"

"Made a big splash, killing that Mex," the kid said.

Watching Reno's face go poker blank, Jason sensed the gambler's mind working.

"I heard a lot of it was luck," Reno said.

The kid's interest flared. "Where'd you hear that?"

"After I got here a few days ago. I went nosing around up in Mex town where it happened. The Mexes don't mention it much, but I talked to one who did. One who claimed that Carmona had emptied his gun shooting at targets, just before Savage shot him down."

McCleod looked surprised. "First time I heard that."

"That's what this Mex said," Reno said.

"By God!" the kid said.

"You think you could take him, kid?"

"I know I can!"

"Now wait just a minute!" Jason said. "Reno, don't be talking this boy into anything. I saw his old man die up in Cheyenne. I don't want to see it happen to him."

"You want a quick rep, don't you, Frank?" Reno said.

The kid gave him a short nod. Reno could see the excitement in his eyes. Reno was getting a kick out of needling the kid's ambition.

"Too bad you don't have some money to bet on yourself," Reno said, "You could maybe double your stake, Frank."

"Hell, I got some money! Won four hundred dollars in Socorro at faro. Quit my job right then, and headed this way."

"How much of it you got left?" Reno said.

"I got it all."

"I could maybe get some townsmen around here to cover it. Folks in Rosario are right proud of Savage, it seems."

"Cut it out, Reno," Jason said.

"McCleod here, he could hold the stakes," Reno said. He turned to Jason. "Hell, McCleod, a thing like this could bring in bettors, fill your place here with customers wanting to talk about it. All excited and buying drinks. You could hold the betting slips, and charge a commission off the top."

Jason took on a thoughtful look.

Frank Hatch said, "You mean, set a day for me and Savage to meet?"

"Sure," Reno said.

"And how would you bet?" the kid said.

"You may be good, kid. Maybe as good as your old man was. But I'd have to bet on the hometown boy. But it'd be an even money bet. I got a feeling you *are* pretty good." Reno paused. "You want to bet on yourself, I'll cover it. Four hundred bucks worth."

Jason was wondering if the kid could really shoot. For a brief moment he was tempted to offer his clock pendulum as a target, he was that driven to know. He fought down the crazy notion.

Jason said, "The thing is, Frank, we don't rightly know if your shooting is as good as your draw."

The kid turned to face the clock.

"Hold it, kid! I'll take your word for it!"

"Clock wouldn't be much use without a pendulum," the kid said.

You couldn't argue that, Jason thought. But years of serving behind a bar had made him cynical. He'd heard a mile-deep amount of bluster in his day.

The kid said to Reno, "You want to match my four hundred, we'll gave it to McCleod here to hold." He pulled out a fold of currency from his pocket.

"Sure," Reno said. He took out a wallet, and counted out some bills, and both handed theirs to Jason.

"Wait a minute!" Jason said. "We got to build up interest in this, so's me and some others can get money down on the outcome."

Reno said, "I like fast action." He paused. "What do you say, kid, we give Jason here ten per cent of the loser's half for holding the bet?"

"Why not?" the kid said, and turned to leave. "It'll be out of your half, not mine."

"What's the big rush?" Jason said.

The kid was already at the doors.

"Going to double my money in a hurry," the kid said. He disappeared and the doors swung back behind him.

"Hell," Jason said, "he don't even know what Savage looks like."

"Yeah," Johnny Reno said, starting to follow. "I'll have to point out Savage to him."

"Cold-blooded bastard!" Jason muttered, watching Reno leave. "I shouldn't have took their bets to hold."

He didn't know the kid, but he recalled he'd liked the kid's old man, up there in Cheyenne in the old days.

He reached under the bar and brought out a bottle of his best stock and poured himself a drink and downed it. It was something he seldom did this early in the morning.

"Goddam Reno!" he said.

Out on the portico, Reno caught up with Hatch who had stopped to survey the street. Impulsive damned kid, Reno was thinking.

In the back of his mind was another thought. Impulsive as the kid was, it wouldn't do to let him take Will Savage by surprise. Not when Reno had four hundred dollars riding on Savage.

And, if there was any way Reno could better Will's chances, he'd better be working on it.

With a crazy kid like Hatch, anything could happen.

Reno began to sweat a little. That four hundred he'd given McCleod to hold was most of his grubstake. He'd better make damned sure he didn't lose it.

"Where do I find Savage?" the kid said.

"Hard to tell. He moves around town a lot, doing odd jobs."

"Odd jobs? With his reputation?"

"He's not taken to hiring his gun," Reno said.

"Must be stupid."

"Those are the kind you go to watch out for, Frank."

"I'd be obliged," the kid said, "if you'd point him out ot me. I'd like to get this over with."

"Sure," Reno said.

A figure caught his attention, coming into the main street a half block away. He appeared to be carrying a bucket of paint in his left hand, and had a step-ladder hoisted on his right shoulder.

Reno swore under his breath, squinting to see if Will Savage was wearing his gun. He swore again, seeing that he was. Ever since he'd killed Carmona, Will was seldom seen without it. Had he been unarmed, Hatch couldn't, according to custom, open fire on him.

"That him?" the kid said.

"No," Reno said. "That's not him."

"You're a liar," the kid said.

Reno, in desperation, said, "I'm telling you it isn't!"

Will kept walking toward them. He was now only fifty yards away.

"Hey, Will Savage!" the kid called. He stood with his legs spread, and his hand near his gun.

Will stopped.

"Draw, you sonofabitch!" the kid yelled.

Will let the ladder fall.

Reno could see his four hundred going.

He was standing just to the right of the kid, and he kicked out as the kid's gun cleared leather.

His kick landed behind the kid's right knee just as he squeezed the trigger.

The bucket of paint spurted white through a bullet hole, as it went flying from Will's left hand.

The kid fired again as he recovered his stance. He missed. Will didn't.

The kid spun around to face Reno as Will's slug slammed into the right side of his chest.

For a split second, Reno thought he saw accusation in the kid's eyes before he fell.

The shots brought men rushing out of stores and the hotel.

Reno was glad the action had happened on an empty street. He hoped nobody had witnessed the kick he had delivered.

But it had been a close call. He should have waited for a demonstration of the kid's shooting before taking the bet.

Still he was sure Will could have taken him without help had he not been burdened with the ladder.

The nearest of the gathering men now reached him where he stood beside the body of the kid.

"Who is he?" one of them said.

"Name of Hatch," Reno said. "Was figuring on calling out Savage when he found him."

"Looks like he did."

"Dead certain."

"Will take a bullet?"

"One," Reno said. "In that can of paint he was carrying."

Will reached them just then, walking slow, carrying the ladder on his shoulder again.

"Hatch, you say?" another townsman said. "Any kin of old Two-Gun Gus?"

"His son," Reno said.

"Reckon he didn't favor his pa too much, ability-wise."

"I wouldn't say that," Reno said. "A bit to the side and a couple feet higher, and he'd have hit Will's heart instead of his paint bucket."

"Something to think about, ain't it?" the townsman said.

Will stood there, a puzzled look on his face. He stared down at the body. "Who was he? Don't recall I ever stepped on his toes," he said.

"Gus Hatch's son," Reno said. "He was looking for a rep, is all. Said so earlier, and I was following him, trying to talk him out of it."

"I wish you had've." Will said, his puzzled expression

turning to one of real concern. "I surely do hate to be killing folks." He paused. "Particular, folks I never even met."

"Goes with being a gunfighter," somebody said.

Will stared at the man who said that. "Ain't sure I like that part. Ain't like being a part of a book. I feel a mite sick to my belly."

"Come on over to McCleod's, Will," somebody said. "We'll buy you a drink. It'll help settle your stomach."

"Can't," Will said. "I got to go paint the Widow Lavender's kitchen."

"Hell, didn't you just paint it last month?"

"Yep," Will said. "But seems like I just can't get it done to suit her."

Somebody chuckled. "Might be she's taken a fancy to you, Will."

Will appeared to give this a brief thought. "Well, she is, for a fact, a mighty friendly woman."

Braddock, the undertaker, arrived just then. He looked down at the corpse. "Couple of you men haul him to my place."

Two of them picked up the kid's body and started off. Blood and other liquids dripped from it, spotting a trail through the dust.

A bunch of the men headed for the saloon to drink and talk it over. The merchants who had to tend to business returned to their shops.

Reno went along with the crowd.

McCleod was standing on his porch as they approached. His eyes sought out Reno, who was in the lead.

Reno caught his stare and was surprised at what he saw there.

Jason turned then and went inside ahead of the patrons. For a while he was busy setting up drinks, listening to the men's talk about what happened out there on the street.

When a moment came that nobody was calling for a refill,

he caught Reno's attention and jerked his head toward his office in the rear. He headed that way, and Reno followed.

Inside, he went to a safe in the corner, turned a dial, and took out the money that had been bet. He came back and handed it to Reno.

"There, goddammit!" he said.

Reno counted off ten per cent of the loser's half and handed it back to him.

Jason took it, but he held the bills dangling in his fingers as if he was holding a dead snake.

"Forty bucks," he said. "For the kid's life."

"If you don't want it," Reno said, "you can give it back."

Jason hesitated, then folded the money and shoved it into a pocket. He went then to his desk, opened a drawer and took out a bottle of his private stock, and a couple of glasses.

He filled them and shoved one across to Reno. He lifted his own and tossed it off in a gulp.

"Drink up and get out," he said. "I don't want to talk to you."

CHAPTER 6

HOLT sat at his desk in the front of the Record. He had a writing tablet before him, and from time to time he wrote with feverish intensity, then sat back to scan what he had written. Leafing back now through several pages, he reread:

> *And now, as word spread throughout the Territory of Will Savage's conquest of the feared Chango Carmona, another shootist rode into Rosario.*
>
> *He boasted a name known to all: Hatch.*
>
> *For he was the son of the notorious gunfighter, Two-Gun Gus Hatch. Trained by his father from the time he could hold a gun, he was a formidable figure in his own right.*
>
> *When he came to Rosario, he had one purpose in mind. He came to test the prowess of Will Savage.*
>
> *"Where is this man the Mexes call El Salvaje?" he demanded to know, as he approached the bar of the local saloon. . . .*

Holt thumbed through the following pages until he came again to the account of the gunfight as he had just written it:

> *When word reached Will Savage, he was conferring with the six members of the Rosario town council, now convened to consider hiring him as marshal, as Rosario to date had no law officer in residence.*
>
> *"Gentlemen," Savage was saying, moments before he was interrupted, "I consider it an honor to be made this offer. And I will consider it most sincerely. I will let you know of my decision before sunset of this day."*
>
> *All members of the council stood, as the meeting ended.*
>
> *And, at this moment, a resident of the town broke in, breathless with hurry and excitement.*

"Mr. Savage, sir!" he said. "A noted gunfighter, by the name of Hatch, is on his way here to challenge your ability with weapons!"

"To challenge my ability, eh?" Will Savage said.

"Yes, sir. Such were the intentions he announced only moments ago, before he left McCleod's bar."

"Then I must not keep him waiting, must I?" Savage said, showing briefly his handsome smile. He turned to the members of the council who now stood aghast at the fearful news. "Gentlemen, as I said, I will give you my answer this evening."

With that, and a nod to the breathless messenger, he stepped out onto the street to meet this latest challenge.

A trace of his smile was still on his lips.

Holt slapped the manuscript down on his desk top. As he did so, Gloria entered the office from the pressroom.

"What's the matter?" she said. "The novel going badly?"

"It's what I'm doing to Will. It bothers me. A great deal."

She stared at him. "The way you're building him up, is that it?"

"Can't you see what's happening? Carmona was a fluke. But it drew Hatch here to test him."

"So?"

"Hatch was more grist for the mill that grinds out the growing legend of wild Will Savage."

"The legend will grow now, even without your help."

"Yes," he said. "But every word I write makes it grow faster. Can't you see where it could all lead? There'll be others like Hatch. More rep-hungry fools."

"They'll get only what they deserve."

"How can you be so cold about it? Hatch was just a kid."

"He should have had more sense."

"Should have? Of course he should! But he told McCleod he was only eighteen years old! At eighteen, how much sense could he have?"

"It was either Will or him," Gloria said. "Would you have it the other way?"

"Of course not." Holt cleared his eyes and brought his fingers up to massage his forehead. After a moment he dropped his hands letting his fists strike his desk top.

"Dammit!" he said. "Can't you see what we're doing?" He paused. "Sooner or later, some killer will ride in. Some slick professional and Will won't have a chance against him.

"I have a lot of confidence in Will," Gloria said. Her voice remained cool.

"Because you want to have," he said.

"Yes," she said. "Because I want to have. Because I want to believe there is a man in this town who can stand up to Rufe Canton when he comes back."

He stared at her. "All because he stripped your dress down," he said.

"He may as well have bared my breasts, the way rumor has it," she said. "Breasts bare in the sunlight for every lusting male in Rosario to see."

"And for that you'd risk a man's life?"

"For that, a *man* would be willing."

"You think Will is that man?"

She gave him a hard smile. "I *know* he is."

"Poor dumb bastard," he said. "God help him!"

"Don't put it all on me," Gloria said. "You don't fool me. You've got a hope of your own in this."

"Yes," he said. "And God help *me*, for that!"

There was a touch of scorn in her voice as she said, "But if you keep building Will's reputation high enough. Rufe may not come back. That's it, isn't it?"

"I wish I could believe that."

"Go ahead and believe it," she said. "It could happen." She turned abruptly then, and went back into the pressroom.

He sat there, feeling the sting of her words.

He looked again at the novel's account of Will's meeting with the town council. His consideration by them as a prospective town marshal was pure fiction.

But the thought stuck persistently in his mind.

Well, why not? he thought. Rosario needed a lawman in residence. And it would add to the stature of the town. He might try to persuade the council with those arguments.

Walt Judd, the livery owner, was the head of the council. He'd be the man to see.

Holt put on the flat crowned Stetson he usually wore, and stepped out onto the street.

Several doors down, he could see a wisp of smoke rising from above the stables, and guessed that Judd would be using his forge. Judd did some minor smithing, as well as being hostler.

The day was hot, and Holt didn't envy him that job.

As he entered the stables throughway, Judd looked up, and stepped away from the forge where a horsehoe was reddening in the coals.

"Howdy, Holt," Judd said. "You looking to rent a horse?"

"No," Holt said. "It's something else, Walt. Council business, really. You being the head, I figured I'd make my suggestion known to you, to present to the others."

Judd took off his leather apron, and nodded toward his small office up front. He led the way in and sat down. "Fire away," he said.

"I've been thinking it's about time we had a lawman in Rosario," Holt said. "A town marshal."

"What for?"

"Might give more stature to the town. Another thing is that we may get an influx of trouble makers now."

"Like that kid, Hatch?"

"Exactly. And I'm afraid there'll be more like him."

"Who'd you have in mind? For marshal, I mean."

"Only man here who qualifies is Savage," Holt said.

"Well now, I don't know," Judd said. "We've got along for a lot of years without one."

"Things are changing, Walt."

"So I've noticed," Judd said. "And, dammit! Bret, it all

began when you wrote that accusation of Rufe Canton. You'd
ought to have known better. You've brought trouble to the
town; now you want us to hire a marshal to try to keep it
under control. I don't think the council will go along with
the cost of hiring one."

"Suppose I pay his salary."

"Can you afford that?"

"It wouldn't be much," Holt said. "It would be basically a
part-time job. Will would work cheap, I know, on that basis.
You pin a star on him, it'll make him happy, and I can pay
him enough to satisfy him."

Judd gave him a searching look. "Bret, you got a personal
interest in this?"

"Like what?"

"Like having a protege of yours wearing the star when
Rufe Canton comes back."

Holt was a long time answering that. Then he said, "It
wouldn't hurt any to have some law here if he does."

"*When* he does," Judd said.

"You sound damned sure."

Judd shrugged. "Way I see it, you got only one chance he
won't—that's if he gets hisself killed up there in Colfax
County."

It was something Holt did not like to hear. He shoved it
out of his mind and said, "Will you call a meeting of the
council?"

"Yes, I'll do that for you," Judd paused. "But we get a
marshal, we'll need a jail. And that old adobe hoosegow on
the edge of Mex town hasn't been used in fifteen years.
Needs a lot of repairing."

"If you give me an affirmative answer," Holt said, "I'll put
Will to work on it."

Judd gave a slight shake of his head. "You making him
famous has sure made him a friend of yours it seems."

There was a note of rebuke in Judd's remark that annoyed
Bret, and he said, "He considers it a favor, I suppose."

"In his case, I'm not so sure," Judd said.

"What do you mean by that?"

"I mean that you've turned him into a target, of sorts."

"That wasn't my intention."

"We all know that. Still, there's a lot of criticism directed your way."

"I haven't been hearing it."

"Sure you haven't," Judd said. "Ain't many folks got the nerve to criticize you to your face. After all, you did step out onto that street to face up to Rufe Canton. Ain't every man would have had that kind of guts."

"I guess not . . ."

Judd continued, "Now, I guess everyone is waiting to see if you'll have guts to do it again, considering how it turned out the first time."

With some sarcasm Bret said, "And how are they betting?"

"I don't know of any bets."

"No?"

Judd took a while before he answered. "You want the truth?" He paused. "The truth is there hasn't been any money saying you will."

"I take it, you feel like the rest of them."

"I guess so. Hell, you'd be a damn fool if you did." Judd paused again. "In fact, you'll be a damn fool if you're still here when he comes back. Bret, why the hell don't you run? Go back east where he'll never find you."

"I don't know," Holt said. "I don't know why I don't."

Judd shook his head slowly, as if he found this hard to believe. Then he shrugged. "Well, you still got time to decide. I guess. Provided Rufe don't show up unexpected like."

"An unsettling thought," Holt said wryly. "Call the meeting, will you?"

"I'll send word around to the rest of the council; see when we can get together. I'll let you know. You'll want to address them personal, I suppose?"

"That I will," Bret said.

CHAPTER 7

IT was the next day before Judd came over to tell Holt that the meeting had been set for that evening at seven o'clock.

"You better argue well," Judd said. "I had to mention what the reason was for the special call, and there wasn't a hell of a lot of enthusiasm."

"It's not going to cost them anything," Holt said.

"I told them that. But I reckon they're some suspicious when there's an offer of something for nothing. You know that some of the council don't always agree with your editorial opinions."

"Wouldn't expect them to," Holt said.

"Just so you know."

"I know."

"Be there at seven, then."

The six council members, including Judd, represented a cross-section of the business men of the town. Besides Judd, there was Henry Turner, who owned the mercantile, Mike Kelly, the hardware, George Hawkins, the saddlery and harness shop, Sam Braddock, who was the druggist as well as undertaker, and Jason McCleod, the saloon owner.

The council customarily met in the back of the mercantile, not having a regular meeting hall. Turner had closed the store for the evening, but he crossed to the front and opened the door for Holt as he arrived promptly at seven and tapped on the glass.

"Evening, Henry," Holt said.

"Evening, Bret." Turner gave him a speculative glance, but said nothing more.

Turner and Holt pretty much agreed on most things.

Together they approached the others at the rear, who were sitting in a half circle around a pot-bellied stove, not used in this season.

Holt nodded, got a nod or two in return, and questioning looks from the rest.

As council head, Walt Judd briefly stated what they already knew: Holt's reason for requesting this meeting.

"So," Judd said, "I turn the floor over to Bret for further comments, and for questioning by the council."

Holt stood a little to one side of the stove, facing them.

"First off," McCleod said, "I've got a question. Holt, what's your *real* reason for wanting to hire Will as a lawman?"

Holt said, "I'll say here the same thing I said to Walt: The town has reached a point where it needs one."

"That's your opinion," Sam Braddock said. "But then, you've always been opinionated." There had been coolness between him and Holt for a long time.

Jason McCleod picked up on it. "The town needs one, Holt? Or you need one?"

"What's that supposed to mean?"

"Just what I said. I get the feeling you'd like to hide behind Will, and that you think pinning a lawman's badge on him might make him a stronger shield."

"That's a strong accusation," Holt said. "Just who am I supposed to need a shield against?"

"You know damn well who," Jason said. "Rufe Canton, that's who!"

"Is that the way you figure it?"

"That's my guess," McCleod said. "Standing behind a bar you hear a lot of comments made. Like maybe Rufe put the fear of God into you. Pretty soon you begin to put two and two together."

Holt said, "It doesn't always add up to four."

"Only if *you* are doing the adding," Braddock said.

"Sam," Holt said, "my point in suggesting this is to prevent more killings. Of course, you being the undertaker, I can see why you might object."

Hawkins said, "Holt, that's a mean statement to make."

"Sorry," Holt said. "It slipped out. You have my apology, Sam."

Sam Braddock glowered. He was not accepting the apology. "What makes you think that having a town marshal will keep the glory-seekers from coming in?"

"The badge. It's worked in a lot of places. You pin a star on a gunfighter, and it changes the way people see him. Look at Hickock, Bat Masterson, Wyatt Earp, and the like, wearing the badge in the Kansas railhead towns. That piece of tin added something to their statures, held off most challengers."

"And Hickock died up in Deadwood, shot in the head from behind."

"After he'd taken off the badge, Sam. That's the difference."

"Will Savage isn't Hickock," Braddock said.

"Wearing a star, he damn well might be. With that piece of tin on his chest, it may stop fool kids like Hatch from getting ideas."

"That reminds me," Braddock said, "I'm still owed some money for burying Hatch. Who's going to pay it?"

Jason McCleod reached into his pocket and pulled out the folded currency handed to him by Johnny Reno for holding stakes. "I am," he said, and shoved it out to Braddock, as if he had waited too long to get rid of it.

"You?" Braddock said, but he took the money, quick. "How come?"

"Let's just say I knew his old man a few years back," McCleod said.

They all stared at him. They knew Sam had sold the kid's horse.

After a short pause, Braddock turned to face Holt again. Now, his scowl was gone and he seemed less belligerent.

Holt thought, Beats all how getting a bill paid can improve a man's disposition.

"According to Judd here," Braddock said, "you'd pay Will's wages."

"That's right. Like I said, it would be pretty much a part-time job, and I think he'd work cheap."

"You reckon he could fit it in?" George Hawkins said. "It'd take away some of the time he's been spending on the Widow Lavender's kitchen."

He guffawed at his own joke, but nobody else did.

Holt gave them a sweeping glance. "Well, what will it be?"

"I move we give it a try," Judd said.

"I second the motion," McCleod said. "Let's put it to a vote."

"Hold on!" Braddock said. "I move that Holt leave before we do that."

"Why?" Holt said.

"Because you being here could cause undue influence on some members that might want to vote against you. Some who might fear reprisal in your columns of the *Record*."

Judd said, "Bret?"

"Holt nodded. "Might be best. Not for what Sam says, but just so nobody can later make that claim."

He turned away and started for the door, followed by Turner who let him out.

Walt Judd called after him, "I'll let you know of our decision tomorrow."

"I'm looking forward to it," Holt called back.

But he wasn't at all sure this was so. He knew Braddock, for one, was dead set against him. And Braddock's opinions carried considerable weight in the town.

Perhaps more than his own.

He was surprised as well as pleased when Walt Judd came to the office to tell him the council had consented, by a majority vote, to accept his proposal.

"Did it go easily?" Holt asked.

"Four to two," Judd said. "Braddock was opposed, of course. One other, not Jason. But Sam Braddock swings considerable weight in this town. He's ten years up on you, in age and in length of time he's been in business here."

"He's held a grudge for a long time," Bret said, "For some comments I made in the paper during the Lincoln County fracas."

"You've got a way of causing yourself trouble with your opinions sometimes, Bret. Might be well to go a mite more cautious." Judd paused. "I'm thinking back to the Canton thing."

"Hard to change a leopard's spots," Holt said. "But thanks for your help in getting the council agreement. I'll talk to Will right away."

"Good luck," Judd said, and left.

Will stopped by later that day, as he still did occasionally to say a few words to Gloria. Whatever he had going with the Widow Lavender, he didn't let it interfer with this. And Gloria, for reasons of her own, always welcomed him.

Since it didn't seem to interfere with her work, Holt couldn't find any real reason to forbid it, although he made no attempt to hide his irritation.

Today, though, he was glad to see Will, and stopped him as he entered the front door.

"I want to talk to you, Will."

"Sure, Mr. Holt."

"How'd you like to be the marshal of Rosario?"

Will gave him a stunned look. "Me? Marshal?" he said.

"It'd be mostly part time, Will. We couldn't pay you much."

"Would I get a badge to wear?"

"Sure thing, Will. A shiny, nickel-plated star."

"I'd still have some chores I got to do," Will said.

"We—the town council, that is—would see you had plenty of time for those. You'd really only be on call for emergencies." Holt paused. "For that, we can pay you thirty dollars a month."

Will said, solemnly, "I accept, Mr. Holt. And I want to thank you again for all you've been doing for me."

At that moment, Gloria stepped in from the pressroom. "Accept what, Will?"

Will smiled and said, with some pride, "The town council has just hired me to be the marshal."

Gloria's eyes went to Holt, and held there. "Is that a fact?" she said to Will.

"Yes, ma'am," Will said. "Mr. Holt just now told me."

"I didn't know Mr. Holt was the spokesman for the council," Gloria said.

"Walt Judd brought the news earlier," Holt said.

"Your idea, Bret?" she asked candidly.

"Do you object?"

She hesitated, then said, "No, not really. It may be one of your better ideas."

"Glad to see we agree on something," Holt said.

She turned back to Will. "Congratulations!"

"Thank you, ma'am."

"Now that you are marshal, I wish you'd stop calling me 'ma'am'. Call me Gloria."

"Why, I certainly do thank you, ma'am," Will said. "That's the first nice thing to happen from my new hire."

She looked again at Holt, and said, "Will, let's hope it isn't the last."

"I hope it isn't," Will said. "I surely do." He paused. "And now I guess I'd best get along to the Widow Lavender's place. She told me yesterday to come back this afternoon. Said she'd be needing me again."

Gloria frowned, gave him a searching look. "To do what?"

Her sharp tone caused Will to flush. "She didn't rightly say, ma'am."

"*Gloria,* dammit!" she said.

Will looked shocked by her language. "Ma'am?" he said.

"I said to call me Gloria!"

"Yes, ma'am," he said, "I surely will. But I got to go just now."

He nodded then to Holt and strode to the door.

He had a manful stride, Gloria was suddenly thinking.

At the door he stopped and turned to face Holt. "When will I be getting the badge?" he said.

"Soon," Holt said. "We'll have to order one from Socorro."

Will nodded again, and stepped out onto the street.

Gloria kept looking after him.

Holt didn't like what he was seeing in her eyes.

A badge was ordered by Holt from a large hardware dealer in Socorro, and within a week or two it arrived.

Holt prevailed upon Walt Judd, as head of the council, to present it to Will as he swore him in, in a brief ceremony, *to uphold the law and maintain the peace.*

The swearing-in took place in Judd's livery stables office, and was witnessed by both Holt and Gloria.

The badge, as Holt had promised, was a shiny, nickel-plated star. Gloria, personally, pinned it on Will's shirt front.

Then, driven by an impulse, she raised her face to his, and kissed him.

Holt and Judd, both, stood in shock.

Holt expected to see Will flush, but he didn't.

Will took the kiss with a calm pleasure.

As if he was not unaccustomed to such treatment by her, Holt thought. By God! Will was changing fast in some ways!

It was Holt who flushed. With anger.

Surprisingly, Will did not immediately wear his marshal's star at all times. While he was about his hired-man chores, he kept it in his pocket. Only when Holt and Judd took him over to the old native *calabozo*, and explained that part of his new job was to salvage it from disrepair did he don the symbol of his new authority.

He seemed to have decided that he'd wear the lawman's badge only when he was on lawman business.

This was not in keeping with Holt's intentions, and he objected. "Will, you've got to have that star showing always."

"Why?" Will said.

It was the first time Will had questioned one of Holt's directions, and it surprised him.

He said, "Because we are trying to put forth the idea that Rosario is a law abiding town, that it will tolerate no more violations of its peace. You and that star serve to warn away any violators. Do you understand?"

"Why, I reckon so, you putting it that way," Will said. He paused, then surprised Holt again by saying, "You think maybe it'll warn away Rufe Canton?"

"We can hope, can't we, Will?"

"I ain't scared of him," Will replied. "Not no more."

Holt was silent, thinking this over. Then, finally, he said, "That's good, Will. I'm glad to hear it."

And, dammit! he thought, he *was* glad to hear it.

So Will took to wearing the star continuously.

Seeing this, even as he labored at his non-official chores, that townspeople of Rosario were not inclined to laugh. Will, lately, seemed to cast a bigger shadow as he strode the sunlit streets.

At a chance meeting with Walt Judd, Holt remarked on this. "He walks tall now. Like he really believes in himself."

"That's what you wanted, wasn't it?"

"I suppose."

"Bret, I think he's come to believe all that bull you've been writing about him."

"The way he's playing the part, I'm starting to believe it myself."

"Don't do that," Judd said. "It could be fatal."

"For who?"

"For the both of you—when the day comes."

"What day?"

"Rufe Canton Day," Judd said.

"You make it sound like a day of memoriam."

"It could be just that," Judd said. "And the whole town knows it. They just don't know when."

Holt tried to involve himself again in writing his novel, trying to lose himself in the fictitious events which he could therein control.

He had now changed the title to *Man with the Star*.

But he had come to an impasse. Couldn't write anything. He had fallen into a state of lethargy wherein his well of imagination had run dry.

The manuscript lay untouched on a far corner of his desk.

Sam Braddock still seethed over the fact that the majority of the council had voted against him, favoring Holt's suggestion to hire Savage. It was, he felt, an affront to the importance he'd believed he held among his peers. Only George Hawkins, the tack and saddlery dealer had joined him.

Braddock was a man who reacted bitterly when his opinions were contradicted, and he was always driven to even a score.

In the days following the council's decision, he kept searching for a way to hit back at Holt.

Holt was busy in the pressroom when word came that Rufe Canton had left the stalemated land grant war in Colfax County, and had been seen leisurely making his way south.

The word was brought to Holt by George Hawkins.

"I thought you'd want to know," Hawkins said.

Gloria, who was present, said, "Somebody see him heading this way?"

Hawkins nodded. "Stage driver said one of his passengers mentioned seeing Rufe a few days back in Las Vegas, and heard him say he was riding down to Rosario to take care of some unfinished business."

"He sure it was Canton?"

"Who knows? I'm passing on what I heard. Sam Braddock was the one who talked to the driver."

"Braddock! He could be lying."

Hawkins shrugged. "Whether you believe it or not is your business." He turned to leave. "I thought you should be told."

"Thanks," Holt said.

"Sure."

As he left, Gloria said, "Can you believe him?"

"Hawkins?"

"Him, too. But I was thinking of Braddock."

"Like I said, he damned well could be lying."

She nodded. "But it has you worried, doesn't it, Bret?"

He didn't answer. He didn't need to. She could read the answer in his face. It disturbed her. She was surprised that she cared. She knew then that she had warring feelings about him.

She wanted, suddenly, for the message to be a lie.

But suppose it *was* true?

"Did he fall for it?" Braddock said.

"Appeared to," Hawkins said. "I ain't so sure about the girl working for him."

"It'll do my heart good to see the son of a bitch sweat," Sam said. "He's the one brought it all on himself." He paused. "And all the trouble on the town, too. He had a lot of nerve making a smart crack about me wanting killings so's to increase my undertaking business."

"I reckon he meant it as a joke, Sam."

"So is this. A joke on him."

"That's why I got in on it. I like a good joke."

"A sense of humor is a valuable asset," Sam said. "But there's not many of us undertakers got one."

"You want me to spread the rumor around town?"

"That's my intention. It'll be the fun part—watching how he acts with all the eyes upon him."

When Hawkins left, Braddock let his thoughts run rampant.

As usual, when he did this, those thoughts eventually ran toward Gloria.

Ever since her arrival in Rosario he had thought about her.

And when she went to work for Holt, he began living in a state of aggravation. Jealousy, was the word, he admitted freely to himself.

Braddock had wanted her from the time he'd first seen her on the street. A seasoned bachelor of forty, his feelings first upset him, then settled into a deep longing that he had not felt in fifteen years. It was a reawakening of the lusts of his youth that rode him now as a kind of pleasurable pain.

The fact that thus far, in the time she had resided in the town, she had given him little more than an occasional casual nod, had not yet discouraged him. But now, unaware of the strained feelings between her and Holt, he hoped the rumor he'd started would drive Holt to react less-than-heroically and lessen his stature in her eyes.

He had assumed, as had most of the townsfolk, that there was a romantic relationship between them. After all, hadn't she nursed him back to health when he lay almost dead from his multiple wounds?

Just thinking about that aroused his jealousy.

CHAPTER 8

THE five hardcase riders approached out of the north.

"Town up ahead," the one called Pedroza, who was native to the Territory, said. "Is called Rosario, I think."

Buck Hollister, who was the oldest and had gray hair and thought he was the leader, said, "They got a bank there?"

"I don't know," Pedroza said.

"You want to make a deposit, Holly?" Slade asked. His tone was sarcastic, as always, and irritated Hollister.

Hollister addressed the Mexican again. "Any law here?"

"Never been, I don't think," Pedroza said.

"You don't know much, do you?" Slade said.

"I only been there maybe one time." Pedroza's voice was civil, but his black eyes smoldered.

Mott and Bonner, riding on Hollister's left, exchanged glances, and Mott, who was closest, said, "Why you asking, Holly?"

"You ever hold up a bank?" Hollister said.

Mott hesitated. Then, as if he could not tell a lie, he answered, "Maybe."

"What the hell kind of answer is that?" Slade said.

"I ain't admitting nothing," Mott said.

They rode in silence a few paces before Slade said, "You got it in mind to hold up a bank, Holly?"

"I'm thinking on it."

"Rustling is our business."

"Rustling is hard work," Hollister said. "A man reaches a certain age, he ought to look for an easier line maybe."

There was no immediate comment from any of them on that. They had just spent several weeks on on an ill-fated

59

rustlng venture that had left them exhausted. Worse yet, it had left them broke.

They had rustled a herd of Mexican beef from across the border, and driven it up to Fort Cohorn, where an accommodating quartermaster had made a prior agreement to purchase it.

But when they made delivery, they'd encountered a replacement officer with lower business ethics and higher morals who merely confiscated the herd as contraband and threatened to arrest Buck and his bunch if they protested his failure to pay.

Fearful of incarceration, they had left empty-handed and discouraged and in near-desperate straits.

Now, Slade said, "Holly, if you're intending to rob a bank, you'd best let Mott advise you on it. None the rest of us know how."

Mott was the most recent recruit to the bunch.

Hollister glanced at Mott and saw he looked ill at ease. Buck thought maybe Mott didn't know how either.

Slade said to Hollister, "Well, how about it?"

Hollister said, "Let's get up there in the shade of that mesquite and talk about it."

They rode over to the almost nonexistent protection from the sun and dismounted. Sprawled there on the hot ground, tempers frayed, they waited for Hollister to start the discussion.

"It'd be a quick way to pick up a stake," he said.

"Let's hear what Mott says," Slade said.

Mott looked at Hollister. Hollister nodded.

"The best thing to do with a bank," Mott said, "is to scout it first."

"What you mean by that?" Slade said.

"I mean you had ought to look it over careful. Look over the town, too. Size up the temper of the folks as is living there."

"Makes sense," Hollister said. "But we can't do that. We'd

arouse too much suspicion, being a bunch of strangers in a small town."

"What you got in mind then?" Slade said.

"To do it at all, we've got to just ride up to the bank, go in and rob it," Buck said. He paused. "And come out and make our getaway."

"Sounds easy," Slade said, his sarcasm back. "Holly, you already just took us through a rustling scheme that failed. I ain't too confident in following you on another."

"You're free to ride," Hollister said. "We can take that bank with four men just as well as five."

Slade scowled again. "I didn't say I wouldn't do it. I just said I wasn't too confident."

"Robbing a bank is like any other line of endeavor," Hollister said. "To be successful, you've got to put your heart into it."

"Your book-learning words ain't as convincing as they once was. You gave us the same kind of talk before we rustled them cattle up out of Mexico."

"I told you to ride, if you want. It's these others here I'm talking to."

"How much you think they got in that bank, Pedroza?" Slade said.

"I told you, maybe they don't got a bank."

"You hear that, Holly?" Slade said. "Maybe *they don't* got a bank."

"If they don't," Hollister said, "we won't rob it."

The Mexican laughed, his black eyes watching Slade.

"You find that funny, Pedroza?" Slade said.

"*Si. Muy comico.*"

"You damn Mexes got a queer sense of humor."

Pedroza lost his smile, but he kept staring at Slade.

Slade stared back, then his eyes fell under the obsidian glare of the Mexican. Slade was tough, but that glare suddenly chilled him.

That was one reason Slade did not try to wrest leadership

from Hollister. All the others except the Mexican were disenchanted with Holly now. Pedroza liked Hollister, hated Slade. Pedroza would side with Hollister in a confrontation.

Slade knew he'd made a mistake in needling Pedroza, but it was too late now to change that. He could tell that by the look in Pedroza's eyes.

Hollister was speaking again. "I don't have to tell you we're broke. And if they've got a bank, there's money there."

For a brief spell nobody said anything. They were thinking over what he's said.

Then Pedroza said, "I think maybe I remember they got a bank." He paused. "I hope they got."

"Well?" Hollister said. "Do we do it?"

Nobody answered him.

"Goddammit!" Hollister said. "Let me put it this way: Anybody against it?"

Nobody answered this either.

"Then it's unanimous," he said. "And I don't want to hear any of you bellyaching later. Let's go!"

The first thing Holt did, after he got word that Canton was coming, was hunt up Savage. He found him working on the jail.

Will was well along on the repairs to the old native *calabozo*. He still hadn't come to the point of calling Holt by his first name. "Howdy, Mr. Holt."

Bret gave him a quick nod, and said, "Word is there's trouble coming, Will."

"Trouble? What kind of trouble?"

"Rufe Canton trouble."

"Well, we always figured that," Will said.

"I mean *now*."

Will gave him a blank look. "What?"

Holt told him quickly what Hawkins had said. ". . . You being marshal now," he said, "I thought you ought to be the first to know."

Will gave him a long, studying look. Then he said, "So! You want me to take care of him for you."

Bret couldn't bring himself to answer that. Instead, he said, "I just thought you ought to know."

After a short silence, Will said, "Sure. And I'll be on the lookout for any trouble comes to town." He paused. "Might be, though, if you was to help—I mean two guns might be better than one. Just in case I need a backup."

It was Bret's turn to be silent. He wanted to speak, but was finding it hard to do so. Finally, he said, "Sure, Will. I've already taken to wearing my gun." He flipped back the top of his coat to reveal his Shopkeeper's Colt in its shoulder holster.

He saw something like relief flicker across Will's face. He's getting smarter fast, Holt thought. He's beginning to have some sense.

Holt wasn't too sure he liked that.

The facade of the Stockman's Bank wasn't impressive. It was one door west of Main Street at the intersection of Bowdre, facing north, and nestled between two other storefronts: one the corner structure which housed Kelly's Hardware, the other a seamstress-shop.

It differed inside, in that it had a metal teller's cage fastened to its short counter a few feet in from the door. And further back, behind the cage and in a small room off the bank manager's office, there was an iron-doored vault where the cash was stored.

The manager and owner of the bank was J. Phillip Fontaine, who'd once run cattle over on the Pecos, until he'd got smart and sold out and started up his bank three years ago.

He was doing better than fair in this new business. Which was, he thought ruefully, about all you could expect in a town like Rosario. Most of his business was with outlying ranchers whose problems were familiar to him, as a former cattleman himself.

He did have, of course, a monopoly on the town merchant banking as well.

Now, seated at his desk in his comfortable office, he was a reasonably contented man, in his middle forties, and glad to be free of the sweat and uncertainties of a rancher's life.

From where he sat, through an open door he could see the back of his young clerk and teller, Tom Ford, as he sat behind his cage window engrossed in some of the endless paperwork that went with his job.

A capable young man, Tom, Fontaine was thinking. Fontaine shoved off on him as much of the record keeping as he could. He also saw to it that Ford swept out the place daily, although periodically, for the heavier janitorial duties, Frontaine sent for the town's general handyman, and now part-time marshal, Will Savage.

Fontaine was taking his ease in his swivel chair, purchased some time ago in Santa Fe. He was at the moment bothered only by a pesky fly that droned insistently around his nodding head. And once again he was sleepily congratulating himself on his change of occupations. A swivel chair beat a rocking saddle by a country mile, he was thinking.

Over at the *calabozo* on the edge of Mex town, Holt and Savage were still talking.

Savage said, "Maybe I best leave off work on this jail cell and go hang around your office, on account Rufe might come riding in."

"Maybe so," Holt said. "Although there's no word of when he might get here."

"Even so," Will said.

"Yeah, even so," Holt agreed. He tried to hide just how much he wanted Will with him.

Will tossed his tools into a corner of the old adobe cell, and locked the door.

"I reckon them tools'll be safe there," he said. "I never heard of nobody breaking *into* a jail."

Holt glanced at him. Will's face was serious.

"Yeah," Holt said.

Together they walked back and entered the gringo part of Rosario. They entered by way of Bowdre, and just as they neared Main, Will stopped.

"I just remembered I was supposed to see Mr. Fontaine about washing them bank windows," he said.

"Go ahead," Holt said.

"Whyn't you step in with me for a minute?" Will said.

"All right," Holt said.

They entered. Tom Ford stood behind his window cage and looked up from some papers. He was a serious faced young man.

"Gentlemen," he said.

"I was supposed to see Mr. Fontaine," Will said.

"Sure," Ford said. He moved to the counter gate and opened it.

Will and Holt both went through and moved toward the door to Fontaine's office.

Young Ford heard Fontaine's voice as he greeted then.

Buck Hollister called his men to a halt as they reached the outskirts of the town.

"Now, all of you remember what I said. We ride in, find the bank, get the money, and ride on out. And we do it fast."

"Sounds easy," Slade said. "What do you think, Mott?"

"We ain't sure there is a bank."

Hollister cursed. "Don't go confusing the issue!" he said. "Let's go!"

"Eeeaaay!" Pedroza yelled. He kicked heels to his horse, shot into the lead, thought better of it, and reined up.

"Damn fool!" Slade said. But he caught the look the Mexican gave him, and didn't say anything more.

Buck Hollister led them in at a trot.

Tom Ford first saw them as they pulled up in front of the bank, dismounted and tied to the hitchrack. Even through the window grime he could tell they were a lean and range-hardened bunch. Strangers. The gray-haired one, though, had a faintly aristocratic look. A rancher and his hired hands, Ford pegged them as, although it bothered him that he knew none of them by sight.

He retreated to his cage and waited, further bothered when the door opened and three of them trooped in. It shouldn't take three to accomplish bank business, he thought.

A sudden suspicion struck him. He half-turned away in the direction of Fontaine's office.

"Hold it right there!" Buck Hollister said.

Ford stopped and turned back. "What can I do for you, sir?" he said. His voice cracked a little as he said it.

"I want to make a withdrawal," Hollister said.

"You have an account here?"

Hollister didn't answer. Instead he pulled a gun from a hip holster and leveled it across the counter, pointed at Ford's chest. He nodded toward the rear office. "Anybody back there?"

"Just Mr. Fontaine," Ford said. A second later he was wishing he hadn't lied.

"Call him out," Hollister said.

Ford turned again toward the rear and took a step.

"I said to *call* him," Hollister said.

The three men were staring coldly at him now. Ford lost his voice.

"Well?" Hollister said.

Ford made a try. "Mr. Fontaine, sir!" he called. "Oh, Mr. Fontaine!"

Gloria came into the *Record* front office, placed a small cardboard sign in the window to indicate the office would be closed for a few minutes.

She went out, locking the door behind her, and headed up the street toward the bank. She carried in her purse a small bundle of currency that Holt had asked her to deposit for him when the bank opened. He had other errands to attend to, he had said.

As she walked toward the corner of Bowdre, she saw the five mounted strangers reach it from the opposite direction and turn in.

Her first thought was that Rufe Canton might be one of them, and she quickly felt through the fabric of her purse for the hardlines of the little .25 caliber pistol she was carrying there. She had gone armed with it ever since she'd heard the rumor of Canton's possible return.

Satisfied that one of them was him, she relaxed and gave them no more thought until she reached the intersection herself.

She was a little surprised then to see the five horses at the tie rail, saddles empty. Only two of the dismounted riders were visible, standing one on either side of the mounts.

They appeared to be watching opposite directions along Bowdre. The one watching east, a Mexican, spotted her at once and kept his eyes on her as she neared him.

She was not unused to having men watch her, and did not entirely dislike the attention either, but all that changed when he grabbed her and clamped a calloused hand over her mouth.

Banker Fontaine had appeared in his doorway in answer to Tom Ford's call.

"What's the problem?" he said, irritably.

Then, as he saw the armed men just beyond the teller, he was struck by sudden fear. Still in the doorway, one hand dangling at his side, he wagged the hand to try to warn Holt and Savage of possible danger.

"Some gentlemen here to see you," young Ford said in an unsteady voice.

Fontaine thought fast. If he stepped out to meet them, he'd be in their hands. He had not been a tough old cowman for nothing.

"I'll be at my desk," he said. "Send them in."

He turned abruptly then, to get back out of their sight.

"All right, bub," Buck Hollister said. "You heard the man. Let us in."

Ford moved like a sleepwalker to the counter latch, released it and lifted the top.

Hollister started through, just as Pedroza came in, prodding Gloria ahead of him. Mott, who was nearest the door, said, "Wait a minute, Buck. We got us a visitor."

Buck halted and turned back. "Goddammit!" he said. "Why didn't you hold her outside?"

"I been afraid she scream," Pedroza said.

"All right," Buck said. "But keep her quiet." He jerked his head toward the teller. "And keep an eye on this one."

Inside his office Fontaine reached his desk and grabbed a gun from a drawer. He faced Holt and Savage who were watching, and silently mouthed the word, "Robbers!"

They each drew weapons and took position to either side of the doorway. The banker dropped into his chair behind the desk, holding his own pistol ready but out of sight.

Hollister burst into the office with Mott and Bonner at his heels. All had guns in their hands.

Fontaine, Holt and Savage all pressed triggers together.

Fontaine's gun failed to fire. But Holt's and Savage's didn't. Their bullets ripped into Hollister, driving him back against his cohorts who wheeled and fled as he dropped in the doorway.

Savage leaned into the opening, blocking Holt, and fired four fast shots that dropped the fleeing pair.

Pedroza rushed for the outer door, dragging Gloria with him. Holt and Savage, each afraid of hitting her, held their fire.

Outside, Slade was already mounted, but in his panic had forgotten to untie his reins from the hitchrack.

Pedroza's mount, spooked by the shooting, had somehow broken loose and was running wildly down the street.

Pedroza let go of Gloria, grabbed for Slade's reins, jerked them loose and tossed them up to Slade. Panicked, he then reached for the cantle and tried to pull himself up behind.

But Slade spurred the horse, shaking the Mexican loose, and started racing away.

"*Hideputa!*" Pedroza said. "Son of a whore!" He pulled his gun and drove Slade out of his saddle with a bullet in the back. The horse kept running.

The Mexican turned then as Savage came out of the door.

For one brief second the two faced each other. Then Savage, reacting quicker, triggered his weapon. The hammer fell on an emptied chamber.

Pedroza grinned.

And Gloria shot him in the heart with the pistol she'd wrested from her purse.

Savage was first out, following by Holt. They exchanged glances, after taking in what had happened. Gloria's eyes were on Holt. Behind him, Fontaine was trying to push past.

"Bret," she said, "you know what to say."

He knew at once what she meant, and her coaching brought a flicker of resentment in him. But it passed as he realized he truly was in accord with her thinking.

Fontaine had got to where he could see Pedroza's body, and that of Slade lying in the street. "You got them both, Savage?"

Will started to shake his head, but Gloria said, "That was fine shooting, Will."

Will frowned, opened his mouth to speak, then shut it as Fontaine said, "Congratulations, Marshal! Rosario can be proud of you for this. You killed at least four of them, single-handed."

Holt met Gloria's stare. "Five," he said. "I missed in there."

The crowds were forming up and down the street, brought out of the stores and shops and the saloon by the gunfire. They quickly began to gravitate toward the bank.

Fontaine said, "I hope you will make the most of this as a news story, Bret. And give plenty of credit to the way our bank was protected by our intrepid marshal. I will vouch for what happened here. After all, I was an eyewitness to it all."

"You can be sure I will," Holt said. "Both in the news story and in the next book about Will."

"You can use my real name in that, too." Fontaine said. "I've no objection."

"I didn't figure you would," Holt said.

"And you, Marshal. You can cut five more notches on your gun."

"I never notch my gun," Will said. "Notches on the handle might spoil my aim."

That was a line right out of the first novel, Holt was thinking. There was nothing wrong with Will's memory.

The account of the abortive bank robbery as published in the *Rosario Record* was picked up several days later by the *El Paso Daily Herald* and the *Santa Fe Republican* and a dozen or more territorial newspapers.

They all read pretty much the same:

NEW MARSHAL AT ROSARIO HALTS BANK ROBBERY
Famed gunfighter Will Savage kills five single-handed!

As Holt wrote the news story he let exaggeration take hold, an inclination he could not seem to resist anymore when it came to describing the actions of Will. It was as if he could no longer separate the reality of facts from the fictionalizing of them:

. . . and from the bodies, some identification was taken. Enough to establish that the five outlaws were all members of the notorious Buck Hollister gang of bank, stage and railroad robbers, whose depredations have for years terrorized the western territories.

They were killers all, whose experienced and systematic looting of banks ranked with that of the James boys and the Youngers. . . .

CHAPTER 9

THE stage from Socorro came pounding in, old Josh Butterworth handling the ribbons, sitting ramrod straight on the box.

Two weeks had passed since the shootout at the bank, and each day Holt lived in suspense that this might be the day Canton would arrive.

Now, as the team and coach passed the *Record* office and pulled a halt in front of the hotel, Holt's stomach was tying up in knots.

True, the stage came from the west, not the north. But who could be sure of the direction Rufe might come?

He watch with fear as the passengers disembarked.

Two men got off, dressed in city attire. With them they had several pieces of luggage, besides a valise each.

The only other passenger was Ezra Steiner, a man of varied business interests who had taken the stage out a couple of days after the bank shooting.

Now, as the two strangers entered the hotel, Steiner left his own valise on the porch and came hurrying toward the newspaper office.

Holt stepped outside.

As Steiner, who always seemed on the verge of excitement, drew close to where Holt waited, he called out, "A couple of your colleagues, Bret! A big town reporter and a news photographer!"

"From Socorro?"

"Bigger than that," Steiner said. "From El Paso."

"You must have talked up the bank episode pretty strongly."

Steiner grinned. "It was heavy news. And I had a clipping of your *Record* account with me. It got me a lot of free drinks for the telling, in Socorro. From there the story travelled fast, it appears. It didn't take long for this pair from El Paso to jump on it."

"What are they doing here?"

"They'll be interviewing you shortly," Steiner said. "Looking for more details. And pictures."

Holt nodded. Then he said, "You hear anything about Rufe Canton's whereabouts?"

Steiner shook his head. He gave Holt a searching look. "Well, I thought I'd tip you off about the newcomers."

"Yeah," Bret said. "Thanks."

As Steiner went back up the street, the El Paso pair were already leaving the hotel and starting down. One of them was carrying a camera and tripod on his shoulder. The other had a case of what were probably photo plates.

Not wasting any time, Holt thought, as he waited.

The big, florid one with the case was in the lead, a rotund man in his forties.

"Are you Bret Holt?"

Holt nodded.

"I'm Lucas, reporter with the *El Paso Daily Herald*." Lucas shoved out his hand, and Holt shook it. "The young fellow there with the camera is a *Herald* photographer. Name of Sid Farr."

"What can I do for you?" Holt said.

"My editor sent me to get a story firsthand on what's going on up here."

"You've read my account of it?"

"Of the bank shootup, yes. No doubt that local dude just rode in with us told you. And I'd appreciate further details you can furnish. But I'm after something more than that." Lucas paused. "Holt, I've been reporting for a lot of years. And I sense a bigger story behind this somewhere."

"Such as what?"

"For one thing, this Will Savage character you've built up. Oh, I've read one of your novels, and discounted a big percent of it. But now—" Lucas broke off, shaking his head— "now we're told he singlehandedly shot down the whole five members of the notorious Buck Hollister gang of bank robbers."

"That's right."

"Your local friend told us on the stage ride up here of some earlier shooting encounters. This Savage is the man who killed Chango Carmona? And killed Two-Gun Hatch's son in a street duel?"

"The same," Holt said. "And we made him the marshal here just before Buck Hollister made his try on the bank."

"A damn lucky move on your part, I'd say."

"I guess we all agree on that."

Lucas said, "I've got to admit I never heard of the Hollister gang. In fact, I never heard of Buck Hollister before." The reporter's eyes searched Holt's face, probing. "This isn't some more of your hyperbole, is it?"

"Ask around," Holt said. "Most anybody can tell you of the bank holdups pulled off by the Hollister bunch. Banks, stages, trains, you name it."

Lucas frowned. "You're avoiding my question. Of course there are plenty of stories *now* crediting Buck and his men with crimes not already ascribed to the James boys and others." Lucas paused. "I discount most of it. And I'll tell you why: I talked last week to a drifter familiar with the border country. Bought him drinks, as a matter of fact. He claimed to've rode a time or two with Buck. Buck was nothing but a two-bit rustler, he said. Buck's game was never more than stealing cattle in Mexico and running them up to our military forts and selling them to Army quartermasters."

"A man could have two trades," Holt said.

"Not one as hard as rustling Mexican beef," Lucas said. "Not if he was good at one as easy as bank robbing."

Holt said, "Well, I might have exaggerated a little. But you know how that is—you're a reporter yourself."

"True. But I don't make up pure fiction and call it the truth. Still there's more than one way to make a story big. Your way is one. Another is an exposè of fraud."

"Strong words, friend Lucas."

"Exactly."

"My guess is you didn't bring your photographer all the way to Rosario to take *my* picture," Holt said.

"I hope you'll bring Savage around to meet us."

"Of course."

"And we do want some shots of you. You *were* involved in the shootout. And the girl, too. Imagine the fight she must have had! Almost taken hostage by the Mexican, and saved by the fifth and final shot of Savage!"

"She's working in the pressroom," Holt said. "Shall I bring her out?"

"Please." Lucas was staring up the street now. "And that man coming toward us, wearing the star, he is the marshal? Will Savage, himself?"

"That's him," Holt said. He turned into the office to get Gloria.

Will came up to the men from El Paso, and halted.

"You're Savage?" Lucas said.

"Yes, sir."

"I'm Jay Lucas, from the El Paso *Daily Herald.* And this is Sid Farr, my photographer."

"Pleased to meet you," Will said. He shook hands with both of them.

A moment later, Holt came out with Gloria.

The reporter from the *Herald* gave her a curious stare. He grinned slightly and said, "You underwent a terrifying experience, Miss Gloria."

Gloria frowned. "Vestal," she said. "Gloria Vestal."

"Miss *Vestal,*" Lucas corrected.

"Yes," Gloria said. "And if it weren't for the prowess of our town marshal, it would have been worse. Far worse. Few men could have risked the shot that killed Pedroza. Not when he was holding me as a shield."

"An expert shot," Lucas said.

"I would say so, Mr. Lucas."

The reporter turned to Will who was standing there in silence. The marshal looked more disturbed than flattered, Lucas thought.

"You must have much confidence in your ability to shoot straight," Lucas said.

"I been getting a lot of practice lately," Will said.

"So I've heard." Lucas said. "I'd like to get the story of the bank holdup direct from you, a little later. And right now my photographer, Sid there, is ready for some pictures, if you'll oblige."

"I got no objection," Will said.

Sid said, "First, let's get one or two of Holt, the girl, and the marshal together."

"I'll want individual shots of each, too, Sid," Lucas said.

"All right."

Farr set up his tripod, draped a black cloth over the back of his camera, and stuck his head under the hood. He withdrew again and said to Holt, "The three of you get a little closer. And Miss Vestal, you stand in the middle between the two men."

They changed positions, while Farr eyed them critically, then disappeared again. "That's it! Don't move!" His words were barely distinguishable under the hood, but they all stood frozen with expectancy. "One, two, three!"

He reappeared. "That was fine, folks. Now we'll get some individual pictures. Let's start with you, Miss Vestal."

A crowd had formed on either side of the street, but kept back out of the way, a little awed by what was transpiring. It was all new to the people of Rosario, seeing how a team from a big town newspaper worked. They watched with fascination.

"You are a fine looking woman, if I may say so, Miss Vestal," Lucas said softly. He reached out to touch her, with the pretense of positioning her to pose. He gave her arm a squeeze before moving away.

Sid Farr checked under his hood, then came out and said, "Give us a big smile now."

"Why?" Gloria said. "What's to smile about in this story? A bank was almost robbed, and five men were killed. It isn't something I'm inclined to smile about."

"But it's routine," the photographer said. "We always ask a pretty woman to smile."

Gloria said nothing.

Farr stuck his head under the cloth again. There was a silence, then his muffled voice said, "You're not smiling, Miss Vestal."

"No, I'm not," she said.

"Dammit, Sid!" Lucas called. "Take the picture! The girl is right."

The shutter moved, and Farr came out. His face showed pique at having his professional judgment challenged. Silently, he changed plates.

Lucas came over to Gloria and patted her shoulder. He faced Holt and said, "Now you!"

Holt made his way to in front of the camera. He stifled a grin at the expression on Gloria's face as he passed her. She wasn't a girl you laid hands on casually. Something Lucas would find out soon if he kept trying it.

"I suppose you want *me* to smile," Holt said to the photographer.

"Of course not," Farr said. "You were an active participant in the gun battle."

"And Miss Vestal wasn't?"

"Exactly," Farr said.

Holt looked over to catch Gloria's reaction. She showed none, just as he expected.

Whatever her feelings at the moment, she wasn't about to

reveal her own killing of Pedroza. He knew she would hold to her intent to build up Savage's reputation because of her lust for retribution over what Rufe Canton had done to her.

Farr spent little time on Holt's pose. He wanted to get on to Will as his subject.

"Now," the photographer said, "last, but not least—I want several shots of Marshal Savage. By himself."

"How you want them?" Will said.

"First, we'll take one with you facing the camera, Marshal, in your best fighting pose."

"Fighting pose?"

"You know, crouched a little and with your gun drawn."

"Like this, maybe?" Will said, trying to oblige.

"I think so," Farr said. "Let me look." He ducked under the black cloth. A moment later he brought his head out again. "Lower your gun a bit, Marshal. Like you'd be shooting from the hip."

"I don't ordinarily shoot from the hip," Will said, "less'n there's no help for it."

The photographer looked surprised. "You don't? Why is that, Marshal?"

"If you was to point your finger at something," Will said, "would you do it from your hip?"

"My finger? Well, of course not!"

"That's the way I shoot mostly, Mr. Farr. I just hold the gun and point it like it was my finger, and squeeze. That way I most usual hit what I'm looking at."

"Do say," Farr said. He looked a little perplexed. "I didn't know it was done that way."

"My way, anyhow," Will said. "And I don't crouch neither."

Lucas spoke up. "It'll be a more effective picture, Savage, if you do it like he says, if you don't mind, sir."

Will didn't say another word. He lowered his gun, and held it hip high.

"Much better," the photographer said. "Makes you look like the *real* Will Savage, gunfighter."

Will uttered something that sounded like an obscenity before he seemed to realize that Gloria was standing only a few paces away. He turned his head and said to her, "I'm sorry, ma'am! I forgot you was there."

"Please!" Lucas said. "Face the camera, Marshal!"

Will grunted something, and resumed his pose.

"Get it, Sid!" Lucas called.

Farr came out from under his hood with a big smile on his face. "You looked downright formidable, Marshal."

"That all you want?" Will said.

"Let's get a good street shot, Sid," Lucas said. "Let's move your camera up the street to the intersection where the bank is, and get a profile of the marshal in his fighting crouch, and staring north like he was waiting the approach of the Hollister gang, and ready to draw."

They all moved toward the crossing of Bowdre Street, and halted just before they reached it.

The crowd on either side moved parallel with them.

Farr set up his camera on the near, inside corner, catching an angled view of Savage as he peered north up Main.

Will looked over to the camera man and Lucas, and said, "Hell, this ain't the way it happened at all. Me and Mr. Holt was already inside the bank."

"Let us take care of this, Savage," Lucas said. "We know what we're doing."

Will shrugged and remained silent.

Holt and Gloria stood as interested spectators.

Will took the pose as directed, and stared northward, crouched with his hand hovering over the butt of his six-gun.

At that moment, and a short block away, a rider on a limping claybank mare turned into the west end of Bowdre.

The photographic scene was hidden from his view by the hardware store on the corner adjacent to the bank.

Rider and horse both looked hard-used, as if they were at the end of a long stint of desperate riding.

Solo Gurk, the rider, dismounted, cursing as he took to leading the mount. The mare, on top of all else, had thrown a shoe, while still a mile out of town.

What was on Gurk's mind at the moment was to find a livery and get the shoe replaced. And that as quick as possible, because there was a civilian posse not too many miles behind him.

A posse was always a risk when you pulled off a robbery alone because a civilian posse was far more apt to take up pursuit of a single quarry than of a gang.

And a civilian posse was more likely to resort to a lynching if a capture occurred. More likely than one led by a lawman, always hampered by duly constituted restrictions.

But Solo Gurk had always been a loner. Which accounted for his name. (Solo was also a corruption of his Christian name of Soledad, given to him by his Mexican mother. Gurk's father was an itinerant gringo cowboy who had drifted out of Solo's life during his early childhood.)

Gurk, unlike the late Buck Hollister, truly was a journeyman bandit with work credits in the Texas Panhandle as well as the Territory. Early the previous day, he had hit the little bank in an unlikely place called Chinos Grandes.

He had done it just as the banker had arrived to open its doors. Gurk had tied up the banker after cleaning out the vault of two thousand dollars, and was outside mounting the claybank for a clean getaway when he was recognized.

Recognized by a Texan cattleman named Charley Deppler, who a year before had been robbed by Gurk of a ranch payroll.

The Texan opened fire, but Solo had escaped.

Immediately suspicious, Deppler had rushed into the bank, freed the banker and got up a posse on his own, since there was no lawman in Chinos Grandes.

Some time later Gurk, pausing to rest the mare after a

climb to a benchland, looked back and spotted the trailing horsemen. He counted six of them, and they were coming fast.

That goddam Texan! he thought. He'd be thinking of his own money robbed that time in the Panhandle, and he would keep on coming.

And so he did, Deppler and his posse. All the rest of that day, part of the night, and starting again at dawn.

This morning Gurk's mare, near run-out, had thrown the shoe.

Luckily, he was near a town when it happened. Gurk thrust away the idea of wasting time getting the exhausted mare shod. Hell, he had money in his saddlebags—he'd buy a fresh horse if he could find a livery, and be well on his way to escape.

Now, plodding east on Bowdre Street, he saw the sign on the Stockman's Bank of Rosario, and recognized it as the name of the place where the Hollister bunch had been destroyed by the gunman known as Wild Will Savage.

The Soledad part of him crossed himself, while the Gurk part was cursing. One thing he didn't need just now was a run-in with the likes of Savage. He'd sneak in, trade for a fresh mount, and sneak away. And he'd not stop running until he crossed the Mexican border.

Thus, engrossed in his thoughts, he plodded into the intersection of Main, passing the wooden structure that blocked his vision.

Too late, he caught the glint of sunlight on metal. He spun toward it and saw the tall man with the star on his chest crouching there, gun in hand.

Gurk dropped the claybank's reins and thrust his hands into the air.

For a long, startled moment, Will stared at him in silence. Then he said to the stranger, "Keep 'em up!"

Will strode across the intervening yards, reached his left

hand out and jerked Gurk's gun from his holster, and shoved it into his own belt.

Gurk said, "You Wild Will Savage?"

"Yep."

"How'd you know about me?"

"I didn't," Will said. "Who are you?"

"You don't know?"

"I'm asking, ain't I?"

"Goddam!" Gurk said.

His eyes swept the men behind Savage and the camera to one side with the photographer's hand resting on it and a pleased expression on the photographer's face.

He saw the girl, then he turned his head to face a whole group of spectators across the street.

"What's going on here?" he said.

"You're under arrest," Will said.

Gurk was silent before he spoke. Then he said, "What for?"

"I don't know," Will said. "What've you done?"

Gurk met Will's level stare. Then he said, "My *mamà* wanted me to be a carpenter."

"A good trade," Will said.

"I should have listened, I think."

Gloria came hurrying toward them, and said, "Don't you think you'd better take him in, Will? You've got the jail in shape. Put him in it."

"Well," Will said, "I don't know what he done."

"The jail, Will," she said softly but firmly." "Until you find out why he surrendered."

Solo stared at her, and said, "I been just a driftng cowboy, took by surprise."

"That horse of yours looks hard-used," Gloria said. "Will, lock him up."

Holt had come over to listen, and now he said, "She's right, Will."

"Dammit!" Will said, "I'm getting tired of folks telling me what to do." He paused. "What's your name, stranger?"

"Gil Martinez."

"You Mexican?"

"With a name like Martinez?"

"You don't look Mexican."

"My mother was a *gringa*," Gurk lied.

"Let's go, Martinez."

"What about my lame horse? And she needs feed, water."

"We'll put her up at the livery."

A look of resignation came to Gurk's face. He thought again of his mother. "*Què serà*," he said. "What will be. I should have listened."

Savage unlocked the door of the renovated *calabozo*. "In you go!" he said.

Gurk stepped in and looked surprised. "Hey, *hombre*, you got a clean jail!" He paused, and his tone changed. "How long you going to keep me here?"

"Long enough to see who's chasing you," Will said, and went out, locking the door.

"Ay, *mamà!*" Gurk said, when he was alone. Somebody would look into the mare's saddlebags, and find the money he'd robbed. He'd be finished, then. Not to mention a few hours from now when the posse followed his trial into town.

Will had built a small lean-to on the side of the jail cell, forming a crude office which he now entered.

He sat at a rough table he had banged together to serve him as a desk. On the table was a writing tablet he had begged from Holt, in which to keep any records he might need.

And now, somewhat laboriously, he took a pencil and scrawled the date, and the name, Gil Martinez, followed by a brief notation: *Held for being suspicious.*

CHAPTER 10

AN hour later the exhausted posse rode in.

By this time the stolen money had been discovered by Will in the saddlebags, and put by Holt and Fontaine into the Stockman's Bank vault.

It was the Texan, Charley Deppler, who spotted the jail and the newly painted sign, *Marshal*, nailed on the adjacent lean-to, as the trail-weary bunch entered the town midway between old town and Rosario proper.

He hauled up, dismounted, and stomped the stiffness from his legs as he approached the office. He found it locked and empty.

There was no sound from the *calabozo* either. Out of curiosity, though, he stomped to the door and peered through the barred opening in the heavy slab.

At first he could see nothing in the gloom of the dark cell.

He was about to turn away, when Gurk, trying mightily to remain quiet, sneezed.

Deppler immediately looked in again, using his hands as blinders to shield out the sunlight from his eyes.

This time he thought he made out the form of a man lying on a bunk fastened to the far wall.

He said, "Who's in there?"

There was no answer.

Quick suspicion struck Deppler. "That you, Gurk, you half-breed son of a bitch?"

Still no answer.

"All right," Deppler said. "We'll see about this, right pronto."

He stomped back to his horse and got into the saddle, and

said to his men, "If they got a marshal here, he's got to be somewheres."

"Good thinking," one of the others said. "What you going to do, Mr. Deppler?"

"Find him, of course, you damn fool!"

"Makes sense," the other said.

Deppler, holding himself tall in the saddle, led the posse into the main part of town.

Will had just returned to the vicinity of McCleod's saloon, after escorting Holt and Fontaine to the bank.

The men from the *El Paso Daily Herald* were inside having a drink, Will believed, and he was about to enter himself, when the trail-dusted posse pulled up at the tie rail. He turned at the commotion.

The tall man in the lead saw his tin star, and called out, "Hold up there, Marshal!"

Will faced him from the porch, his legs slightly spread, his hand hovering near his six-gun. It was the way he had been facing most people who called out to him lately, ever since the shootout at the bank.

Deppler, with a long experience of sizing up men, noted the stance and lessened slightly the hard tone of his voice.

"I'd like a word with you, Marshal."

"Talk away," Will said.

"Maybe over a drink would be better," Deppler said. "We just come off a long ride."

"Right here is all right," Will said. "Long ride from where?"

Deppler held a moment's silence. He wasn't used to having his suggestions rejected. But then he said, "Chinos Grandes."

"Chinos Grandes?"

"A half-Mex bastard named Gurk held up the bank there. We been chasing him ever since."

Will swept his eyes over the posse, then back to the leader.

"I don't see you wearing no badge."

"No, but my name is Deppler, cowman from over that way. You maybe heard of me."

"Can't rightly say I have."

Deppler scowled. "Originally out of Tascosa, Oldham County, Texas."

Savage said nothing.

"Well, goddammit! who you got in that jail of yours?"

"Stranger called Gil Martinez."

"Got kind of a Mexican look?"

"Not as much as the name sounds."

"Riding a claybank mare?"

"It happens he was," Will said.

"That's him! Where's his horse?"

"Judd's Livery," Will said. "Down the street there. You can see the sign."

Deppler turned to his men. "Let's go!" He started to turn his horse in that direction.

"Saddlebags are empty," Will said.

The Texan halted. "That money belongs to the First Bank of Chinos Grandes."

"If so, I intend to get it back to them," Will said.

"We'll take it."

"I don't think so."

"We're the posse, dammit!"

"I don't see no proof."

"You got the proof locked up in jail."

"Gil Martinez?"

"His real name is Gurk. Solo Gurk. Bastard robbed *me* once over in the Panhandle." Deppler paused. "We'll take him, too."

"You can't have him, either."

"I got five men with me, Marshal."

"Same number I had to kill a couple of weeks back," Will said. "You can't come riding into Rosario and start throwing your weight around, Mr. Deppler."

Deppler looked at him blankly. "Rosario? Is this Rosario?"

"Yep."

"Hell, I read about those killings!" Deppler paused again. *"You're* Will Savage?"

"Yep."

"Kind of changes the look of things," Deppler said. "The fact remains, though, our bank was robbed of a couple thousand dollars. And you got the son of a bitch that done it in your hoosegow."

"Two thousand, give or take a few dollars," Will said. "Me and Mr. Holt and Mr. Fontaine, the banker, counted it when he took the deposit of it."

Deppler nodded, and said, "I don't see how you'd object to us taking that thieving son of a bitch off your hands then."

"And the money?"

"You got it in the bank, leave it. We'll let our banker contact yours about a transfer."

"Who's the law in your town?"

"Ain't none. Sheriff, of course, but he's way over in Lincoln. That's why we got us this civilian posse."

"You'll have to get a law officer to take him off my hands."

"No way," Deppler said. "We ran him down, and we'll take him in."

"You said he robbed you personal once," Will said. "I reckon that's make a man resentful."

"What're you getting at?"

"He's my prisoner. I ain't giving him up to maybe get lynched."

"You can trust us," Deppler said. "You can tell we're law-abiding citizens, can't you?"

"Nope," Will said.

"What the hell do you mean—'*No*'?"

"No, I ain't giving him up."

"I ain't accustomed to being refused," Deppler said,

"I figured."

"We're six armed men against one."

"Odds like that, I'm used to," Will said.

A posseman nearest to Deppler said in a low voice. "Listen, Mr. Deppler, I don't intend to get in no shooting fracas with a gunslick like Will Savage."

Another rider, sitting his saddle next to him, agreed. "Me neither!"

"Shut up!" Deppler said. "I got to think about this."

"You do that," Will said. "Meanwhile, I got me some other chores to do."

"Might be," Deppler said, thoughtfully, "we'll just ride out peaceful like. Go find us a U.S. deputy or such like."

"That'd be best, by far," Will said. "And I'd be obliged to you. I surely do hate unnecessary killing."

A third member of the posse spoke up. "Listen to what he's saying, Mr. Deppler."

"I'm hearing him," Deppler said crossly. "I ain't deaf."

"You boys come back when you got a legal authority with you," Will said.

Deppler dismounted and tied his horse to the rack. "I reckon we'll get us a drink or two, put up our horses to get care at the livery, and lay over a spell. That all right with you, Savage?"

"Sure," Will said. "I reckon you got a long ride back."

"Have a drink with us?"

"Not now," Will said. "I promised I'd drop by to see the Widow Lavender. She's got something on her mind."

Deppler gave him a blank look. Then he said, "Maybe later, then." He led the way into McCleod's, followed by his companions.

They stayed quite a while before they came out. The sun was getting low when they mounted their horses, rode to Walt Judd's livery stables and left them there.

They made a camp of sorts a few hundred yards from his corral, as night fell.

They were up with the sun, rousted out the hostler, paid their bills and saddled up.

They rode then to the Pecos Restaurant and had breakfast. Afterward, they rode toward old town. They had spoken as little as possible to the hostler or the man in the restaurant.

They did not ride far. Only to the unattended jail cell.

Will had not yet put a bunk into his improvised office—he was still sleeping in a shed behind the hotel.

Out of sight of Rosario's citizens except for those of the native *barrio*, Deppler and his posse of civilians made no effort to hide their intentions.

They rode up to the cell door. Deppler shot off the lock and shoved the door open. He stepped in with his gun drawn.

"All right, Gurk," Deppler said. "We're taking you back to stand trial."

Gurk peered past him and through the open doorway. "I don't see my horse. You going to make me walk?"

"We'll take turns riding you double."

"It'll slow you down, I think."

"We'll worry about that."

"It's me that worries. I think you ain't going to ride double too far. Like maybe to the first big tree you find."

"Trust me," Deppler said.

"You joke, eh?"

Four of the possemen were crowding around the door now while the other one kept watch.

"Take the bastard!" Deppler said. "Take him and tie him up. He'll ride, slung over a saddle like a corpse, if that's the way he wants it."

Solo knew when he was beat, "Wait! I'm coming."

They trussed his hands behind him, shoved him up to sit a saddle. One of them climbed up behind another's cantle, holding the reins as a lead line.

Gurk kept eyeing the coiled rope on Deppler's saddle. "Come ready, eh?"

Deppler didn't reply.

"Some trial," Solo said.

"You been found guilty," Deppler said.

"That marshal, he ain't going to like this."

"He can cut you down when he catches up."

"He maybe cut you down with that Peacemaker he got," Solo said.

Deppler scowled. "Let's get to riding," he said to his men.

Solo grinned. "Here he's coming now," he said. "Coming this way up the street."

The men of the posse turned in their saddles and stared. It was Will, all right. Walking toward them.

Deppler cursed. "Let's go, dammit!" He kicked his horse and moved a dozen paces before he noticed none of the others were following. "You men hear me?" he hollered.

"We hear you, Mr. Deppler," one of them said. "But we don't aim to be targets for the likes of the marshal there."

Deppler swore again. "You boys been reading too many of them dime novels."

"Ain't the dime novels scare me," the man said. "It's the newspaper accounts."

Will strode up to them and halted. "What you're doing is against the law."

"Like I said before, we're six against your one," Deppler said.

"I put a sixth cartridge in the empty chamber of my gun this morning," Will said. "Just in case."

"You got a hell of lot of confidence in your ability, Marshal."

Will nodded. "Way things been going lately, I reckon I have. Undertaker has come to consider me a friend."

"Jeez!" somebody said. "I don't like this."

"I got some big connections in Santa Fe," Deppler said.

"Mr. Holt told me some about that Santa Fe Ring. Politicians, ain't they?"

Deppler nodded. "And I got friends among them, Savage."

"You put my prisoner back in that cell and buy a new lock for the door, and you'll live to ask them for help," Will said.

"Jeez!" the posseman said again.

"I'm not a gunfighter, Marshal," said Deppler.

"Didn't figure you were. So that don't leave you much choice, does it?"

He turned to the man who kept saying "Jeez!"

"You! Get him off that horse, untie his hands and herd him back into the jail there."

"Yes, sir!" the man said. He dismounted and went to Gurk's side to help him down. He reached for Gurk's tied hands.

And at that moment Gurk drove his spurs hard into the horse's flanks. It bolted, jerking the lead reins from the loose grasp of the surprised man holding them.

Gurk kept roweling the horse, and it plunged through the cluster of possemen and burst free, racing wildly but jerkily as it sometimes stepped on the trailing reins.

"Stop him!" Will yelled.

"Hold it!" Deppler ordered them.

The men sat uncertainly at the contradictory commands. A couple of them started to move out, seeming inclined to obey Will.

"I'm in charge here," Deppler yelled. "I say, let him go!"

There was authority in his voice. He was a man accustomed to giving orders. And a man known to have politico-commerce ties to the Ring, a power in the Territory.

They listened.

Gurk, on the spooked horse, disappeared behind a sprawl of adobe huts.

"Now!" Deppler called. "*Now* we'll follow. But not too close." He set his own mount off at a lope.

They left Will afoot and swearing. He knew Deppler's intention: let Gurk escape just far enough to be out of Will's protection, then catch and lynch him.

A new kind of rage suffused him. He felt duped. He'd let a man in his custody be taken. It did not set well with the self-image he had lately acquired.

He stared helplessly as the posse rode away in the pursuit of his prisoner.

A small crowd of the *barrio* people had gathered a few yards away, attracted by the shot that destroyed the jail lock, and the ensuing altercation.

Will's eyes swept them, stopping on one man in a *charro's* clothes, lounging indolently in a saddle aboard a dapple gray gelding. He was smoking a cigarette, but his stare was intently on the marshal.

Will stared back.

After a moment, the charro said, "Señor *Salvaje*, you want to borrow my horse?"

"I'd be obliged," Will said.

"Then he is yours," the charro said. He touched spurs to the gray, crossed to Will's side, and dismounted.

Will swung up in the saddle and turned in the direction the posse had gone.

"*Buena suerte, Salvaje!*" the charro said. "Beyond that hill is a big, lone tree. I think maybe they hang him there."

Will took off at a run.

A trail of sorts circumvented the north side of the hill, and the floating dust kicked up by the riders assured Will that they had taken it.

The charro's gray was a big, strong mount, and Will was sure he could overtake Deppler's bunch. His problem was what to do when he caught up to them.

He had never been a man to think ahead. His whole life he had acted on impulse. For better or for worse.

Lately it seemed to be for better. He had acquired a lot of prestige in a short time. He was content with the way his life was now going.

Except, of course, at this particular moment.

Still, he wasn't too concerned. Hell, wasn't he Wild Will Savage, *Man of the West, Man with the Star*? Who could beat him?

He rounded the hill, and there they all were. Just as the charro had suggested, crowded around a big oak tree.

They had caught up with Gurk, handicapped as he was with hands tied behind him and reins trailing.

A rope had been flung over a limb and a noose was already around his neck. He sat disconsolately in the saddle, waiting for a quirt to fall on the horses's rump.

Deppler said, "You better kick your feet loose from those stirrups. Else when that horse moves, you're going to have the longest neck in the Territory."

Gurk hastily freed his boots, but he said nothing.

"You got anything to say," Deppler said, "now is the time to say it."

For a few seconds Gurk was silent, thinking. Then he said, "I wish I been a carpenter."

"Nothing else to say?"

"That says it all, you Texas bastardo!"

Deppler looked affronted. "I don't know why you New Mexicans hate us Texans the way you do."

"Slap the horse and get done with this," Gurk said. "You don't understand if I tell you."

Will Savage fired his Peacemaker.

The range was too long for effective shooting, but his luck still held.

His bullet struck the horse of the mounted man who was holding a dally of the rope-end around his saddle horn.

The horse went down, and as it fell the man leaped free, letting go of the rope.

As the rope went slack across the tree limb, Gurk drove his spurs in and his mount shot forward, just as the horse had earlier in front of the jail cell.

But now, besides the trailing reins, there was thirty feet of dragging rope behind Gurk.

With the noose still tight around his neck.

The posse sat their saddles as the horses shied away from the fallen mount. For a startled moment none of them made a deliberate move.

Then, with a curse, Deppler alone took off on a chase after the fleeing man. His eyes were on that dragging rope. He didn't have to catch Gurk, he only had to keep him moving. Sooner or later that rope would snag on scrub brush or rock and do the lynching for him.

Deppler grinned. A broken neck or a strangling, either one would satisfy him. Let nature take its course, he was thinking. It would legally absolve him from blame, he guessed. Not that he was worried about that, not with his connections in Santa Fe.

Savage saw what was happening, and spurred his own horse forward. He swept by Deppler's bunch with scarcely a thought. Nobody tried to detain him—it was obvious his reputation awed them. More so now than before, after his lucky shot.

They appeared to be mostly a merchant bunch, with maybe a couple of town loiterers thrown in, and the early excitement of the chase had long since worn off. They had no intention now of getting themselves killed because of Deppler's stubbornness. Who the hell knew what Wild Will Savage might do, if he was crossed further?

As he closed in on the two of them, Will could see the trailing rope that Gurk, in his desperation, was ignoring. It was only luck that thus far it had not snagged.

And that son-of-a-bitch Deppler, Will thought, he's trying to make it happen.

He drew his gun, sighted beyond Deppler, and although he hated to do it, shot down the horse Gurk was riding.

Gurk, his feet still dangling free of the stirrups, was thrown free. Deppler reined in and turned to face Will as he rode up. Gurk lay stunned and unmoving.

"Well, what will it be?" Will said. "It's you and me, and the winner takes him. I don't have to tell you, your men ain't about to help none."

Deppler's jaw muscles worked as he struggled with his fury. Finally he said, "I reckon I've lost, then. I ain't fool enough to get killed over a half-breed Mex. Maybe the territorial courts will hang him."

"Maybe they will," Savage said. "Meanwhile, you get the hell out of my town."

"I'll get a sheriff's deputy sent out from Lincoln to bring him in," Deppler said.

"No. That ain't good enough. You get a United States Deputy Marshal sent. I ain't releasing him to one of your politicking friends."

"Have it your goddam way then," Deppler said. "But one of these days you may find out I was a bad man to cross."

Savage shrugged. "Maybe I will."

A couple of days later a lawman unknown to Will, but known to Holt, rode up to Will's improvised office and tied up to a post Will had driven into the ground.

Holt, who was talking over recent events with Will, looked out of the open doorway and recognized him. He got up as the man entered.

"Kind of a ways off your beat, aren't you, Deputy?"

"I got a big district to cover, Holt."

Will was staring at the stranger's star.

"Will Savage," Holt said, "meet United States Deputy Marshal Blaze Barker. It isn't often he ever gets to our little town."

Will stood and extended his hand. Barker's hand brushed Will's and quickly withdrew. "You got a lot of fame, Savage," Barker said.

He was a man in his forties, weathered and worn, and looked as if he'd long ago given up smiling. "How much of it is true, and how much is pure bull written by Holt here?"

Will was about to grin, but the humorless look on Barker's face stopped him. His own features grew hard. His eyes met the deputy's and held, but he made no answer.

Holt, watching, felt a sudden chill. By God! he thought, he touched a sore spot on Will there. Will, nowadays, was starting to take himself very seriously.

"I was sent to get a prisoner," Barker said finally. "Request made by Charley Deppler and a banker over in Chinos Grandes."

"You got a warrant?" Will said.

Barker pulled a paper out of his coat pocket and threw it on the crude desk. "Name of Gurk," he said. He pulled another sheet from another pocket. He unfolded it and handed it to Will. "Here's a dodger on him, picture and all."

Will looked at it. "All right."

Barker drew forth still another paper. "And here's a letter from the banker authorizing me to return the money he robbed."

Will scanned papers, then nodded. He said, "You understand I wasn't about to take that Deppler's word for anything."

The faintest lift of a lip lightened Barker's face. "Yeah. I'd have refused him too, was I in your place."

Holt said, "He tried to hang the prisoner after breaking him out."

Barker nodded. "He's got a reputation for being long on lynching, the way I heard it. Goes back to his Panhandle days." He paused. "Well, let's get on with it. We'll see this time that Gurk gets a trial."

Will fished the key for the cell lock from his pants pocket, and led the way out the door. Outside, he turned to see if Barker followed.

Barker said, "No doubt Holt will find plenty of grist for his dime-novel mill in all this." He gave Savage a long, hard stare that seemed to have a trace of envy in it. "You had best not get to believing too much of it."

Will didn't answer him.

CHAPTER 11

SO now, Holt thought, another chapter had been added to the legend of Will Savage.

Almost unwillingly, he was already concocting in his mind the way he would exploit the recent events on the printed page.

This, even though there was always present the nagging awareness that some time in the future it could all bring down disaster on poor Will.

He had acquired a compulsion to color the facts, not only on the pages of the novels, but on the pages of the *Rosario Record* as well.

Now, in his mind, he was seeing the words he had written to describe Will's most recent actions:

> . . . . *and as Wild Will Savage stood at the corner of Main and Bowdre streets in Rosario, accepting the plaudits of its admiring citizenry for his recent annihilation of the fearsome Buck Hollister gang, there occurred a sequel feat of near equal courage. . . . Even as reporters and photographers from distant cities were recording the details of the prior action, another bank robber, fleeing a pursuing posse after robbing the First Bank of Chinos Grandes, rode inadvertently into his presence.*
>
> *With his famous quick-wittedness, the gunfighting marshal instantly recognized the culprit as the wanted notorious half-Mexican desperado, Solo Gurk. Within seconds he disarmed him by shooting Gurk's drawn gun from his hand, and placed him under arrest.*
>
> . . . . *Later, the arriving posse, led by the powerful Texan cattle baron Charles Deppler, broke into the jail where Savage had detained the desperado, and abducted him, intent on administering their own brand of justice.*

But Savage, unplacable foe of crime though he is, would not tolerate summary execution without fair trial. He followed the prisoner's captors, catching up to them just as they placed a hangman's noose around Gurk's neck.

In a further exhibition of his peerless gunplay, Wild Will, without a second's aim, placed a bullet where it severed the lynch rope, saving Gurk from strangulation.

After then disarming the entire posse of Deppler and his five hired guns, Savage drove them from Rosario with the admonition to never return. . . .

Gloria entered the office. He looked up, his mind still pondering what he had written.

"Bret, I've been curious about something: did you really miss?" she said.

"Miss what?"

"Miss with your shot in Fontaine's office. At Buck Hollister."

"There were two holes in his torso," Holt said. "One in his heart, one in his gut."

"And you each only fired once?"

He nodded.

"Then you didn't miss."

"I didn't miss. But I told it the way you wanted."

"It was for the best. Will is our best hope," she said. "You know that as well as I." She paused. "He has grown in stature. He believes in himself. He'll not be afraid when Rufe Canton comes."

"Not like another man you know, eh?" he said bitterly.

"You will admit it's true," she said.

"About Will?"

"About you."

"I couldn't hide it from you if I tried."

"No, you couldn't. Not now," she said.

Still bitter, he said, "You want your revenge, no matter what, don't you? Every time I look at you, I think of the old proverb about hell having no fury like a woman scorned. A woman insulted, it seems, can be filled with the same fury."

"I can never forgive what Canton did," she said.

"And if Will can't wreak the vengeance you want, what then?"

"It is something I've been giving thought to."

"You have a gun," he said. "You killed Pedroza. I guess you might want to try your luck again."

"If I thought I could succeed, I'd do that," she said. For a long moment she stared thoughtfully at him. Then, finally, she shook her head and turned away to enter the press room.

She had been noting that Johnny Reno often took his supper in the dining room of the hotel, usually around six of an evening.

Watching now, she waited in the hotel lobby until she saw him enter. As soon as he was seated at a table, she made her way toward him.

Seeing her approach, he smiled. "Like old times, Gloria," he said. "Join me for dinner?" He did not get up.

She took a chair opposite him. "Thank you, Johnny."

"You've avoided me ever since I arrived here," he said.

"Not intentionally," she said. "It's just that a lot has been happening."

"For old times sake, I expected an invitation, possibly to a home cooked meal."

A waitress came, and they ordered.

When she had gone, Gloria said, "It irked me when you left Tucson without so much as a goodbye."

"Sorry. I found it necessary to leave in a hurry. For professional reasons. Maybe you heard?"

"I heard you killed a man who accused you of cheating at cards."

"Did you hear that he was the cousin of the sheriff?"

"No, I didn't hear that."

"I don't run from men, Gloria. But a sheriff—well, even

though it was a pure case of self-defense, I was looking at some time in a jail cell at least. Being locked up doesn't agree with me."

"I recall you were known to be handy with a gun," she said.

"A minor renown I never tried to deny. It's an asset in my business. Makes most card players a little more hesitant to criticize a deal."

"Unless they have a sheriff cousin? Is that it?"

"That's what happened in Tucson," Reno said.

"Did you ever think of me after you left?" she said.

"Of course I did! Like I said when we met in your editor's office, what we had, a man doesn't forget."

She did not speak for a moment. Then she said, "Nor a woman, either, Johnny."

"But now you have Bret Holt."

She was silent—she did not want to be too quick with her answer.

"Am I right?" he said.

"Not what you may be thinking," she said then. "We do not have an—*understanding*."

"What does that mean?"

"We are not engaged," she said.

"There are other understandings," he said. "Like the one we once had."

"Not that kind, either," she said. "It never got that far with Bret and me."

"His fault, or yours?"

"We were close. Then, suddenly, it all changed."

"Suddenly?"

"You've been here long enough to hear what happened to Bret, the Rufe Canton thing?"

"I've heard."

"And what Canton did to me?"

Her eyes searched his face as she asked. She thought she saw a faint twitch of a smile before he hid it. It angered her.

"He stripped me naked in front of the whole town!" she said savagely.

"Come now," he said, "it wasn't that bad, the way I heard it."

She said, "And where did you hear it? In the saloon, no doubt. Men are still talking about it, aren't they?"

"So?"

"So? So it isn't a thing I can ever live down. It eats away at me. Do you know what an insult like that means to a woman?"

He was a man whose profession had taught him to think ahead, and now his mind reached for her purpose in bringing all this up to him. "You'd like to see him killed, wouldn't you? Rufe Canton, I mean."

"More than anything in the world."

"Are you trying to hire my gun?"

When she didn't answer, he said, "First, Canton would face Holt."

"Bret is no match. He learned that last time—besides, he's lost his nerve."

"So he'll try to hide behind Will Savage."

"Yes."

"And Savage is no slouch with a gun, as we've all come to know."

"You're a gambler," she said. "On whom would you place your money?"

When he was silent, she said, "I thought so."

"So you're trying to get me as a backup gun, in case all else fails. And what would I get in return?"

She held his eyes for a moment, then said softly, "As you said, what we once had is not forgotten."

"Suppose I asked for a retainer?"

"A retainer?"

"Compensation *now* for a commitment to future services."

"I'd have to give *that* some thought," she said. "What I had in mind was favor for a favor done."

"In that case," Reno said, "you'll have to wait for my answer."

"You think about it, Johnny. Keep thinking about the way it used to be between us."

"You know how to work on a man's mind when you want something, don't you? But I guess all women are born with that gift."

She did not take offense at his comment, he saw. And that, too, was something to think about.

Henry Turner, proprietor of the general mercantile, greeted Holt as he entered the store.

"Morning, Bret."

"Morning, Henry. Got a list of groceries here that I need. I'll pick them up later, give you a chance to fill the order."

"Gloria balk at doing your shopping now?"

"Why should she?"

Henry shrugged. "Just joking. Thought maybe she got peeved about something. You know how women are."

"Well, I figured I shouldn't load the added chore on her, seeing she is paid only to work on the newspaper."

"Sure," Henry said.

"You got something on your mind, Henry?"

"It isn't none of my business," Henry said.

"What isn't?"

"Well, the story is around that you and her had a kind of falling out lately, even though she's still working for you."

"How'd that get started?"

Henry shrugged again. "You know how small towns are. Like I said, it isn't none of my business."

"Yeah," Holt said. "Well, fill the order. I'll be back by in an hour or so. Put it on my bill."

"That's something I kind of wanted to speak to you about, Bret."

"What is?"

"Well, you've always been a good customer. Paid your bill on time and all, and I appreciate that."

"So?"

"I was just wondering if, considering the circumstances, you'd mind paying cash until we see how things work out."

"What things?"

"Well, you know what I mean. All this about Canton being on his way and all."

Holt stared at him until Turner began to fidget. "Henry, there isn't more than five dollars worth of merchandise on that list."

"Sure, Bret. I know that. And I wouldn't even mention it, only there's a outstanding balance of over thirty."

"Hell, you've carried me for more than twice that at times."

"It's Canton coming that makes the difference," Turner said. "You're a businessman, too. You ought to see how that is."

Anger showed on Holt's face, but he said, "All right, I'll pay cash from now on."

"I certainly appreciate that, Bret. Of course, there's that balance already on the books?" Henry turned it into a question.

"I'll tell you what I'll do," Bret said, coldly. "I'll include it in my will." He turned then and walked out.

As he stepped out onto the porch, he met Sam Braddock about to enter. It was one of the few confrontations he'd had with the man since his appearance before the town council to plead the hire of Savage as marshal.

Each halted to stare at the other.

Holt still wore the scowl from what had taken place with Turner.

Braddock said, "You're looking in a foul mood, Holt. But then, nobody ever accused you of being easy to get along with."

"I could say the same for you," Holt said.

"What's the matter? Turner asking you to balance your account?"

The words startled Holt. And angered him further, too, as the thought struck that other creditors might be sharing Turner's concern over prospective losses.

He said, "Well, you have no worries on that score. I don't owe you a nickel."

"I'm glad of that," Braddock said. "With Canton on his way."

"Sam," Holt said, "we've had our differences of opinion, going back to whose side we favored during the Lincoln County War. But I never figured you so mean-spirited you'd like to see me dead."

Braddock was silent for a moment. Then he said slowly, "Bret, you do me wrong, saying that. I'm not a friend of yours maybe. But I'll take no satisfaction seeing you killed by the likes of Rufe Canton. Believe that."

Bret's scowl faded. He felt a slight thaw in his feelings toward the undertaker. "Glad to hear you say that, Sam."

On sudden impulse he extended his hand.

Braddock hesitated, then took it and gave it a weak shake.

Then he said, "Glad I ran into you, Holt. I've wanted to talk to you about prepayment."

"Prepayment?"

"Yes. For the costs of burying you. An important man like you shouldn't end up in a pauper's grave."

"Go to hell!" Holt said. He turned abruptly then, and walked away, and left Sam standing there.

Inside the store Turner had heard the discussion between the two out on the porch. Now as Braddock stomped in he saw it was Sam who wore the scowl.

"You two setting off sparks again between you?"

"I tried to discuss advance payment for his funeral costs," Braddock said. "He wouldn't have any part of it."

"He's got a lot on his mind," Turner said. "And was I him, I would, too."

Braddock was silent.

Turner went on, "Besides his worry about Canton coming, I hear him and his girl ain't as cosy as they once was."

Braddock's interest rose. "Is that a fact?"

"That's what I hear," Turner said. "I thought you'd find that encouraging."

"What do you mean?"

"Hell, Sam, you've had a case on that girl ever since she got here." Then, because he thought he might have overstepped himself, Turner said, "Or so most folks around here think."

"What's their falling out about?" Braddock said.

"Nobody rightly knows, I guess. The talk is she kind of blames Holt for her getting her clothes ripped off by Rufe that time—in front of everybody."

Braddock said, "That's one more thing I got against him."

Half-joking, Turner said, "This may be your chance to propose to Gloria, if you're a mind to."

Braddock remained serious. "I just might at that. I've reached an age I'm thinking I been a bachelor long enough."

"A looker like her," Turner said, "could make a man start thinking that way."

Braddock was so busy thinking about it, he didn't answer, only nodded.

A thought now intruded in his mind. A thought he tried to banish, but couldn't. He had told Holt he'd find no satisfaction in seeing him eliminated. He'd meant it when he'd said it. But now, fantasizing about Gloria, he knew it wasn't true.

He had never so much as made a strong overture to her, although he often timed himself to be outside his drugstore when she would be passing on her way to or from work.

He had always been shy with women who were attractive, although he was aggressive in most other facets of his life.

Now, after his discussion with Henry Turner, he decided his time had come to pursue a relationship with her.

Later, he was waiting on the porch of his pharmacy as she approached from the direction of the *Record* office.

As she drew near, he called, "Good evening, Miss Vestal!"

She looked up, somewhat surprised at the forward tone of his greeting. "Good evening, Mr. Braddock. Are you cooling off after a warm day?"

"Indeed I am," he said.

She was about to pass him by, nodding slightly, eager to get home and freshen up. It *had* been a warm day in the press room.

"Miss Vestal!" he said. There was an urgency in his voice that halted her.

"Yes, Mr. Braddock?"

"Do you have time for a word or two with me?"

She gave him a puzzled look, hesitated, but said, "About what, Mr. Braddock?"

"About us," he blurted.

She appeared startled, and that frightened him. It was a mistake, he saw. Just the kind of fool thing a longtime bachelor like himself would say.

"About *us*, Mr. Braddock?"

"Well, I didn't mean that the way it sounds," he said. "What I meant was, well, I've watched you pass by for a year or more now, and I've never really got acquainted with you, and that, Miss Vestal, is something I'd very much like to do."

"Why, Mr. Braddock!" she said. "I never would have guessed it!"

"I'm not easy at addressing beautiful young ladies," he said. "But I want to say I've long admired you."

"Why, thank you, sir."

"I mean to say I'd very much like to know you better."

She was facing him now, smiling faintly, giving him a full appraisal. He was a stocky, middle-aged figure of a man. He was also a man with considerable influence in the town.

She did not find him at all appealing. But she weighed his possible use, and thus chose her next words carefully.

"I'm flattered, Mr. Braddock," she said.

"I meant it sincerely. I would like to be your friend. If I can ever be of service to you in any way—Any problems here in town—"

"At the moment, Mr. Braddock, I am concerned with only one thing: The return of Rufe Canton."

For a moment he was silent, tempted to ease her mind by revealing it was only a rumor. But almost at once he realized that would be self-defeating. For want of a comment, he said, "I'm not proficient with weapons, I'm afraid."

"Of course," she said. "And that is why we now have a marshal, isn't it? Well, good evening, Mr. Braddock." She paused. "For *now*," she added, putting stress on the word to give him hope. She resumed her walk.

His eyes followed her. At least he'd made a start, he thought.

The following morning Will Savage stopped by the newspaper office, looking for Holt, and found he wasn't in.

Gloria heard the bell ring as the door opened, and came from the rear.

Will tipped his hat to her. "Mr. Holt, he ain't in?"

"Not at the moment, Will. Can I help you?"

"Wasn't too important, ma'am."

"Oh?" She had given up trying to make him address her by name.

"No, ma'am. I just wanted to talk some about what we'd do when Rufe Canton gets here."

"You don't consider that important, Will?"

"Well, some maybe."

"Yes, I would think so." She paused. "It is very important to me, Will."

"Yes, ma'am, I understnd how it is between you and Mr. Holt."

"That too. But do you understand how bitter I am toward *Mr.* Canton?"

"Yes, ma'am, I understand that, too."

"You're the marshal now, Will. We're depending on you for protection against that evil man."

"That is my intent, ma'am."

"I'm counting on you, Will."

"Makes me proud that you are, ma'am."

She let her eyes rove over his fine physique, his handsome face. He was an attractive man. He stirred something in her that had been lying dormant for some time.

She said now, "Will, you only once accepted my invitation to visit me at home."

"I surely appreciated the dinner you cooked up that time," he said.

"You never came back."

"I figured it wasn't right, ma'am. On account of Mr. Holt and all."

"What was between Mr. Holt and myself has changed, Will."

"Even so, ma'am."

His reluctance tantalized her. There was something else too. Even though he had pledged himself to protect Bret, she wanted to feel he would be her personal instrument of vengeance.

It was a strange need she had. A need she didn't understand, but only felt. And it was all tied in to the physical appeal he had for her. An appeal that had grown stronger as he had grown in stature. From the first time she'd watched him practicing with a gun she had felt it, and as his skill and courage had been repeatedly shown, she had come to think of him as a knight who would risk his life to avenge her dishonor.

It aroused the female in her to a disturbing pitch.

So that now she spoke to him in a voice husky with her desire. "Come to my house, Will. Come tonight! Please!"

"Might be, I'll just do that," he said. "I recollect you cook a mighty fine meal, ma'am."

CHAPTER 12

SHE was pleased when he did show up at her door that evening. His worn range garb had been laundered. He was clean-shaven, and had just bathed—she could smell the tar odor of the soap furnished by the local barber with the hot tub in the rear of his shop.

But he had always kept himself presentable, she thought, even when he was exclusively employed as a handyman. She wondered now if he was aware of what a fine figure of a man he was. If so, he seemed totally unaffected by it, or even by his rapid rise to fame.

Or was he more aware than most people believed?

He had become something of a mystery to her, and that added to her feminine interest.

She sat with him for a moment in her rented shack's tiny room which served as a parlor.

She said, "Dinner will be ready very soon, Will. I'll have to keep an eye on things in the kitchen till then."

"Yes, ma'am," he said. He had recently bought a new, tan, flat-crowned hat, and now he held it in his lap, turning it absently.

"You must get tired of fixing meals for yourself," she said.

"I mostly eat at the Pecos Restaurant," he said.

"That, too, could get tiresome."

"Yes, ma'am."

"Will, for the love of God, call me Gloria!"

"Yes, Gloria."

"I like to hear you say my name, Will."

"I like calling you by it, ma'am."

"You were a long time coming to it," she said, with some peevishness.

"That's because I thought you were Bret's woman."

"I see."

"I've always thought you a mighty pretty lady," he said. "I take pleasure in looking at you."

"Why, Will!" she said, startled. "You *have* changed!"

"Might be, I have. I been feeling different lately. What with Mr. Holt writing me up famous, and local folks getting to know me as a gunfighter, something happened."

"It has to do with pride, Will," she said.

He nodded. "Reckon it does. Sort of makes a man feel big enough for his britches."

She had a sudden thought that made her blush. She got up and said, "I had best check on the cooking, Will. Excuse me."

"Sure, Gloria," he said.

His eyes were roving her figure as she turned. She could feel them, and her flush grew as she hurried from the room.

Once in the kitchen, she stared absently at the utensils on the stove. Pride was a big part of what made a man tick, that she had always known. How much so was now brought vividly to her.

Holt had once had pride. Now it was gone.

Will had once lacked it. Now it had come.

Each man had become the opposite of what he had been, she thought.

She could make use of that. She was titillated by the thought.

Hurriedly, she began to put the dinner on the table. First things, first, she told herself.

He was a healthy eater, she soon discovered. And why not? He was a healthy man.

"Best meal I've had since the last time I was here," he told her.

"Will, you are always welcome," she said.

"I'll be remembering that—Gloria."

After dinner, she insisted that he not help her with the dishes. "I'll take care of them later, Will. Now, let's just sit and talk."

"I'd be glad to help," he said.

"I insist."

"In that case, I won't object." He smiled.

They returned to the parlor. He took a chair, and she seated herself on the small divan.

The thought occurred to her that she had never before seen him smile. He had always been a serious man. It made her wonder about his background. From where did he come?

It was not proper to ask. And she had things in her own past she would not care to discuss. What had been, had been. It was the present that mattered. The present—and the future.

"Do you have a girl, Will?"

"A girl? No, ma'am, I can't say that I have."

"A strong, handsome man like you," she said. "I find that hard to believe." She kept her eyes on him as she spoke.

Instead of looking flustered, he returned her stare with a level one of his own.

"What are you wanting of me, Gloria?"

She was taken aback by his question. It seemed that his sharpness, too, had grown with his fame. She decided to be frank.

"I think you know. I want you to save Bret, and I want revenge against Rufe Canton. And I think you are the man who can give me these things."

"So!" he said. He arose and moved toward her and dropped beside her on the divan. His muscular body pressed tightly against her softness.

She was shocked. She was pleased, too. She took pleasure in the feel of him.

"And what'll you give in return?" he said.

"Why, Will! I never would have expected this from you!"

"Don't lie," he said. He turned then and took her, roughly, in his arms.

"Oh, Will!" she said. And then his mouth was covering hers.

At that moment, there was a knocking on the front door.

At first she didn't hear it, and then she was strongly inclined to ignore it.

It was Will who broke away. "What's that?"

She got up fretfully, and made her way across the room and opened the door.

Johnny Reno stood there. "Thought I'd pay you a call," he said. His words were spoken thickly.

"I've got a visitor, Johnny."

"Anybody I know?"

"Perhaps."

"Well?"

"Well, what?" She had trouble masking her irritation.

"Well, do you let me in, or do you keep me standing here?"

"This isn't a good time, Johnny."

He was trying to peer past her. "You've got a man in there," he said.

"So, what business is it of yours?"

"I thought we were going to get back together," he said.

"You said you had to think about it."

"That's not what I said at all." He paused. "Let me in, dammit!"

"You've been drinking."

"So, what of it? Let me in!"

Will Savage's voice suddenly spoke from directly behind her. "Trouble, Gloria?"

She turned her head and whispered, "Johnny Reno."

Will drew her aside and crowded forward. "What do you want, Reno?"

"You! What're you doing here?"

"Having dinner. Why?"

"I came calling. Gloria is *my* woman," Reno said.

"She was once, maybe, the way I heard it."

"I aim to make her mine again," Reno said.

"Not tonight, you don't," Will said.

"Big man with a gun, are you? Big enough for Canton?"

"Big enough for you, Reno." Will's voice had a hardness that Gloria had never heard before. "Leave now, or I'll jail you for disturbing the peace."

"Careful, marshal," Reno said. "That star you're wearing isn't big enough to stop a bullet."

"Neither is that gambler's coat of yours."

Gloria spoke up. "Please go, Johnny! Don't make trouble now. You can come back tomorrow evening."

"Ah, hell!" Reno said. "I never could refuse a request from a lady." He paused. "Guess you're right, Gloria. I've had one too many. Doesn't happen very often, you know that."

"I know that, Johnny," she said.

"All right," he said. He turned then and stalked off, a bit unsteadily, but not saying another word.

"Damn fool," Will said.

"Not really," Gloria said, closing the door.

"That gun he wears, can he use it?"

"Yes. He has killed."

"Something to think about," Will said thoughtfully.

"Yes," she said.

He shrugged. He took her by the hand then and led her back to the divan.

"No, not here," she said. "In my room."

With his hand still grasping hers, she led the way. They hadn't gone but a couple of steps, when a rapping came again at the door.

They stopped and Will tried to let go of her hand, but she clung to it. "You have much company?" he said.

"No!" she said furiously. "Almost never!" She did not move.

There was more rapping, insistently now.

"Reno again?" Will said. "I'll throw him in the *calabozo* for sure."

She shook her head, let go of him reluctantly, and went again to the door.

"Ah, Miss Vestal!" Sam Braddock said. "There was a lamp within, but I began to doubt you were home."

"What is it you want, Mr. Braddock?"

"I got to thinking about our earlier discussion, Miss Vestal, and—well, I just could not stay away."

"Why not?" she said sharply.

He appeared taken back by her tone. "Why, I thought I made my feelings known to you when we had our talk. Frankly, Miss Vestal, I am enamored of you."

Impatient with his interruption as she was, she could barely refrain from laughing. "How long have you been a bachelor, Mr. Braddock?"

"Why, all my life, Miss. Vestal."

"I see. You do not have much contact with women, do you?"

"Why, yes, I do. I wait on ladies every day in my drugstore. I have a wide variety of remedies for their complaints, you know."

"Well, Mr. Braddock, I am not sick."

"Of course you aren't! As a professional apothecary, I can tell at a glance that you are a fine young woman in excellent health."

"Thank you, Mr. Braddock. But as a healthy young woman, I am at the moment occupied with an interest that is quite urgent. You must allow me to withdraw from your company at this moment. There will be other times, I'm sure, when we may talk."

He looked disappointed, but took her comment philosophically.

"I'm sure we will, Miss Vestal. Until that time, then."

He gave her what he considered a courtly bow, and turned back down the street toward the center of town.

As she closed the door, Will said, "Maybe I came on the wrong night."

For an answer she moved quickly to him, grabbed his arm and urged him into her bedroom.

A long time later she thrust him from her. There was anger and frustration in her which she did not try to hide.

"I was willing!" she cried. "Oh, I was willing!"

"I know," he said, apologetically. "And I'm damn sorry, ma'am. But the problem is, I spent the whole afternoon with the Widow Lavender." He paused, then went on, thoughtfully, "But I reckon this has taught me what my limit is."

CHAPTER 13

HER anger and frustration stayed with her through a long night after Will, still apologetic, left. It lingered through the next day. She was unusually surly toward Bret when he ventured to speak with her, and he soon left her alone.

He thought sadly: It can never be as it once was between us. And this is a woman I would have gladly taken as my wife. Rufe Canton spoiled all that for me.

All day her own thoughts were on Will, that knighthood figure she had conjured up of Will. Toward evening she had mellowed as a hope grew in her that he might return. Return *restored*, she told herself. Curses on the Widow What's-Her-Name!

She took supper alone, her hopes lessening with the passing hours. And then, abruptly, came the knocking at the door.

Her mood rose, and she moved hastily to open it.

"Evening, Gloria," Johnny Reno said.

"Oh, it's you," she said, without thinking.

He gave her a faint smile. "Is that so bad?"

"No. Of course not. Come in."

As he entered, he said, "You told me I could come back this evening."

"Sorry, I'd forgotten. But you are welcome."

"It isn't often that I overindulge in whiskey, you know that."

"Yes, I know, Johnny. There isn't a lot I don't know about you."

"I suppose. We were together a considerable spell."

He started to take a chair, and she objected.

"Sit here beside me on the couch, Johnny."

His eyebrows raised. "You're making me more welcome than I'd expected," he said, but he seated himself in the chair. "For now, I want to see your face as we talk."

"Why?"

"The thought occurs to me that you're playing a game. And when I sit in a game I alway's study the faces of the other players. Comes with my profession."

"Who would I be playing games with, Johnny?"

"Me, I think. Possibly Bret Holt. And that young, good-looking fast gun who got here last night ahead of me. You as much as told me so when we talked before."

"Is that why you are here now?"

"Yes," He paused. "You told me to think about it. I did."

"Before, you wanted a retainer."

He studied her until she gave him a frown. Then he said, "Did you give one to that young marshal last night?"

She flushed, but she said, "No! Not that it's any of your business. You don't own me anymore."

"I would like to, again."

"You were gone a long time, Johnny. Without a word."

"I told you why I had to leave."

"You could have written."

"That Tucson sheriff was set on avenging his cousin. I couldn't chance a letter falling into the wrong hands."

"That's a feeble excuse, Johnny, and you know it. What happened is this: You are a footloose gambler, and when you got free again, you liked it."

"Why, then, am I trying to win you back?"

"For a some temporary fun, that's why. For a woman of your own, but only until your attention span tires, and the call of the roving life gets too strong for you again. You're like all the rest of your kind, not built for anything permanent."

"Are you?"

"I was well on my way with Bret Holt."

"He's a solid citizen," he said. "An author and a journalist. A settled man." There was no sarcasm in his tone. "So what happened between you?"

"He lost his nerve."

He stared at her. "You hold that against him? After what Rufe Canton did?"

"Because of what Rufe Canton did."

"Gloria," Reno said, "you know what you are? You are a bitch."

"You never called me that before."

"I never realized it till now."

"Does that mean you don't want me?"

"I'm not sure."

"Let's not quarrel," she said. "We can be the same as before, Johnny." She patted the divan. "Isn't that why you came back tonight? Sit here. Please?"

"You *are* a bitch," he said. But he crossed over and sat beside her.

She took his hand and held it close to her.

"So this is the way you hire a gun," he said. "Did you try to hire Savage's this way last night?"

She frowned, but she did not loosen her grasp. "What a thing to say! How could you?"

"Easy," he said. "Gloria, you have become a devious woman since those days in Tucson."

"Things have happened," she said. "Not the least of which was your abandoning me."

"Dammit! I told you it wasn't my choice."

"Wasn't it? You say so, but I don't know if I believe you."

"Does it really matter now?" he said. "You are offering yourself, aren't you? And why? It's your way to hire a gun. At least to try, isn't it?"

"Think what you like," she said, with some anger. But still she pressed his hand against her.

"So! Savage did turn you down last night," he said. "I'm surprised. A young buck like him."

"Will you stop ranting about him? Let's just be together like old times, Johnny. No strings attached."

"No strings attached?" He looked down on her, and grinned. "By God!" he said. "That young marshal must have really left you hanging!"

CHAPTER 14

UNDERTAKER-DRUGGIST Sam Braddock, and his some-time cohort, George Hawkins, the harness shop owner, watched with amusement the worried manner that Bret Holt seemed unable to hide since they had spread the rumor that Rufe Canton was returning to Rosario.

Braddock, especially, was enjoying this. As the rumor spread throughout the town, and open conjecture began among the townsfolk concerning the second meeting, his pleasure grew.

Consensus seemed to be that Holt would try to take refuge behind the gun of Marshal Will Savage. Sam helped this idea along by describing Holt's part in seeking Will's appointment.

Unaware that friction was already there at the time that he started the rumor, he had been hoping it would lessen Holt's image in Gloria's eyes.

Now, there was a division of opinion among the townsmen regarding Will's ability to shield Holt from disaster. Even though Will's recent actions had greatly boosted his reputation, there was much doubt that he would be a match for the detested, but dreaded Canton.

Before long, there was considerable interest in betting on the outcome of such a meeting.

Jason McCleod, the saloonkeeper, offered to hold all betting slips. He figured to benefit both by a commission on winnings and by an increase in bar business as excited patrons gathered in his place to discuss the expected match.

His earlier reluctance to accept a fee following the death

of the kid, Frank Hatch, eroded under the vision of the profits to be made by this showdown.

He was quick to realize that Savage's personal presence in his saloon would greatly enhance his customer draw, and he sent word that he wanted to see him.

In due time, Will arrived.

McCleod had been waiting half the day for him. "Took you long enough to stop by," he said, unable to hide his irritation. It was still hard for him to adjust to Will's growth in stature, from saloon swamper to town marshal.

Will said, "It happened to be one of the days of the week that the Widow Lavender usual has a chore for me."

McCleod grunted. "Nice work, if you can get it," he said.

"Feller ought to make the best of his opportunities," Will said. "Mr. Holt told me that one time."

"You always listen to Mr. Holt?"

"Most always," Will said. "What was it you wanted to see me about?"

"I can give you some part-time work here too, Will."

"I don't reckon I could accept that," Will said. "Wouldn't look right to come back to sweeping floors and cleaning spitoons, me being the marshal now."

"You wouldn't be swamping," McCleod said. "I'd pay you to just hang around and talk to customers."

"Talk about what?"

"Tell them what you'll do when Rufe Canton comes."

"I couldn't rightly do that."

"Why?"

"I don't know what'll happen."

"What'll happen is, you'll have to face him."

"Sure, I know that. I thought you meant would I kill him or not."

Mcleod blinked. Then he said, "Two-bits an hour for your spare time, Will."

"All right," Will said. "But only when I ain't busy with my other chores."

"I'll expect you this evening. Can you make it?"

"Yep," Will said. "I done helped the Widow Lavender all I can, for this day."

When Will walked in at six that evening, a sizeable crowd had already gathered at the bar and the tables.

A few men were playing poker, but even these seemed more interested in Will's arrival than in their late dealt hands.

One of the card players, a drifting cowhand from Albuquerque, gave a long stare at Will as he stood hesitantly inside the swinging doors.

"So that's Wild Will hisself," he said. "Is he really as good as he sounds in them stories they tell about him?"

One of the locals at the table said, "Some of us think so. But up against Rufe Canton, ain't nobody too certain."

"What's Savage and Canton got against each other?" the stranger said.

"Ain't nothing personal between them," the local man said. "But Canton, he swore to come back and finish a job he started on Bret Holt on account of some charges made in the newspaper. And Will, being the marshal now, figures it's his job to protect him."

"How come Holt don't do his own protecting?"

Somebody at the table snickered. "Hell, he tried that once, and ended up looking like a human sieve."

"I seen him up close right after it happened," another said. "And after seeing that, I can't rightly blame him none for trying to hide behind Savage's gun."

"Amen to that!" somebody said. "A man couldn't survive it two times in a row."

"Sounds like this Canton is a real hardcase," the cowhand said.

"Meaner than hell and twice as nasty," a local said.

Will came by the table as he made his way to the bar.

Several of the men called a greeting, sounding like a chorus as they sang out in unison, "Howdy, Will!"

Will looked startled, then nodded and kept moving. He reached the bar as a couple of patrons stepped aside to make room at his coming. McCleod faced him from behind the counter.

"Glad to see you on time, Will." Mc Cleod looked out over the crowd and raised his voice to be heard. "Men, some of you come here from out of town, expecting maybe to see some action. In case you don't yet know him by sight, as well as reputation, this here is Rosario's own, Marshal Will Savage!"

Somebody yelled, "Let's hear it for Wild Will!"

There was a ragged volley of cheers.

Will raised a hand briefly, then dropped it.

The patron next on Will's right said, "Buy you a drink, marshal?"

"Not just now," Will said.

The man looked offended. "Teetotaler?"

"I aim to keep my hand steady."

"That's different. You figure you can beat him?"

"I'm hoping."

The man shook his head slowly. "You gunfighters are a different breed. It don't seem like just hoping would be enough."

"I been through a gunfight or two," Will said. "And I'm still alive."

"So is he."

Will thought about that, then nodded and said, "I reckon you got a point there."

Johnny Reno had made his unofficial headquarters at the saloon, despite the coolness with which McCleod regarded him ever since young Hatch's death. Reno had now decided on which man to place a bet.

He knew Rufe Canton only by reputation, but he was

aware that Savage's killings of both Chango Carmona and Hatch were due to flukes. Hadn't his own interference contributed to the second?

He announced his betting choice to the saloon crowd the day after Will had put in an appearance at McCleod's urging. Will was not present when Reno made his wagering intentions known.

"I've got five hundred says Rufe Canton will be the winner," he said.

There were perhaps twenty men drinking and discussing the expected match, but his words struck them dumb. The size of such a bet was beyond the means of all of them. They simply stared at him.

At that moment Sam Braddock stepped into the saloon. Sam was a man with always an eye out for increasing the goodwill of his drugstore customers, if not those of his undertaking business.

The silence in the place startled him. For a brief interval he stood still, surveying the crowd.

Johnny Reno saw him, and called out, "I've just offered five hundred on Canton to win, Braddock. There doesn't seem to be any rush of takers."

Braddock's mind started working. Only he and George Hawkins were aware that the expected coming of Rufe was no more than a rumor created by himself to discomfit Bret Holt.

He was aware too that Will Savage had become a hometown hero, popular with all of Rosario's citizens. The fact that few seemed eager to back Will's chances against the formidable Canton, did not reflect any lack of sympathy for him. It only indicated an accepted belief in Canton's invincibility.

Here then, Braddock thought, was a chance to promote goodwill for himself without risk of losing money.

In a strong voice, so that all could hear, he addressed Reno. "You're a stranger here," he said. "And Will Savage is a hometown boy. I'll just take that bet."

"All five hundred?" Reno said.

"All of it," Braddock said.

There was a cheer from most of the listeners.

Jason, watching them with interest, spoke up then. "Step right up to the bar, Sam. And you, Reno. Make out your betting slips."

"There's just one thing," Braddock said, seeking to cover himself. "There's a time limit got to be placed on this bet."

"Why?" Reno said.

"I'm not a man likes to have things hanging. If the showdown occurs within the next week, the bet is on. If not, it's off."

McCleod, anxious to hold the bet, said to Reno, "Hell, Canton is due any day now, the way I figure it."

"All right," Reno said.

Braddock, assured now he was at no risk, said smugly, "The sooner, the better, I say!"

"You've got a lot of confidence in Will Savage it appears," Reno said.

"Matter of civic duty," Braddock said, "to back our marshal all the way."

McCleod, looking toward the saloon front, said, "You can tell Will that, Sam. He's coming through the doors now."

Will crossed the room, not seeming to notice that all eyes were upon him. He drew close to the bar and said to McCleod, "I'm clocking in for duty."

McCleod nodded. "Braddock here just bet a bundle on you, Will."

"And who took the bet?" Will said.

Nobody spoke, at first.

Then Reno said, in a flat voice, "I'm a gambler, Savage. Nothing personal."

Will nodded. "Reckon I understand."

"You know that *I'm* all for you, Will," Braddock said. "I'm the one convinced the council to appoint you marshal, you know."

Will stared at him. "No," he said, "I didn't know that. Bret Holt told me different."

Braddock hesitated, then said, "Well, I'll admit that at first I didn't take to the idea. But once I was convinced, I went all out to get you a favorable vote from the rest of the council."

"I'm obliged, then."

"Sam is backing you five-hundred-dollars worth," McCleod said.

"I'll try not to let you down, Mr. Braddock," Will said. "I'd hate to see you lose your money."

Braddock gave him a close look to see if Will was being sarcastic. He judged him to be sincere, and that bothered Braddock a little.

CHAPTER 15

GEORGE Hawkins, the saddlery owner, was in trouble. His business had dropped off to next to nothing.

Cowhands from the surrounding area, riding in for a drink or two at McCleod's place occasionally used to splurge hard-earned wages on a fancy bridle or a down payment on a new saddle. Now they were hoarding their dollars to bet on the outcome of the expected showdown between Will Savage and Rufe Canton.

The amusement he'd figured to gain by helping Braddock monger his rumor had backfired.

He hadn't sold an item since the rumor became rampant.

And it griped him that Braddock's business hadn't suffered. People got sick and bought his nostrums and patent medicines, no matter what.

People also died, requiring burial, in spite of his remedies. In spite of them, or maybe even because of them—Hawkins thought maliciously.

I was a fool to go along with Sam, he thought. Besides being a fool, his conscience bothered him.

Hawkins, unlike Braddock, had no grudge against Holt. He'd taken part in fostering the hoax only because he liked a good joke. Now, it was apparent, the joke was partly on himself. And he did not appreciate the humor.

He made a decision, suddenly, to try to undo the wrong he had helped inflict on Holt—and on himself. To hell with Sam Braddock, with his healthy businesses thriving on sickness and death.

He locked up his deserted tack shop, and headed toward the *Record* office.

Holt looked up from his desk as Hawkins came in the door.

"I've got to talk to you," Hawkins said.

"More news about Canton?"

"Well—yes and no."

"He's here?" Holt's voice cracked.

It struck Hawkins then just how great a toll the rumor had taken on the editor. He felt ashamed of his part in perpetrating it.

"He isn't coming," Hawkins said.

"Not coming! How do you know?"

"I know, because it was all something Braddock dreamed up to harass you. A lie."

Holt said in a hard voice, "But it was you that told me."

"And I'm sorry about that, damned sorry, Bret. I never realized how bad it would wear away on you. I just never put myself in your shoes to think about it."

Holt stared at him, anger rising, but he said nothing.

"Well, cuss me out, dammit!" Hawkins said.

"Goddam your eyes!" Holt said.

"Yeah," Hawkins said. "I deserve that."

Holt gave him a thoughtful scowl. "If you're sincere when you say that, you ought to be willing to make amends."

"How?"

"Walk this town and tell everybody you meet that you were a liar."

"Wait just a damn minute!" Hawkins said. "You're putting that pretty strong!"

"It's the truth, isn't it? You acted as Braddock's lackey."

"I didn't think of it that way, at the time."

"And now?"

"I see it different, of course. That's why I'm here. But I can't do what you ask. Hell, every man who's placed a bet and finds he was excited over nothing, is going to hate my guts."

"So?"

"I've got a business to run in this town. I can't afford to anger my potential customers. You can see that, can't you?"

Holt considered this with a brief silence, then said, "Yes, I guess so. So put the blame on Braddock, where it belongs."

Hawkin's face hardened. "You want me to speak against a friend. I won't do it."

"You don't have much choice." Holt said, still seething over being tricked. "Either you or he is going to take the brunt of the blame."

Hawkins took on a hurt look. "Bret, I didn't think you'd get so hard-nosed when I told you. I made a mistake coming here."

Holt's voice flared. "My God, man! How did you expect me to react? I've been in a continuous sweat ever since the goddam rumor started. And all for nothing!" He paused abruptly. "Never mind, George. I've got a *Record* edition ready to run off the press. It won't take much to add a couple of column inches revealing this was a hoax."

Hawkins showed relief, but he said, "Since I came to tell you, you'd ought to keep my name out of it."

Some of Holt's ire had left him. "Yeah. All right, I'll do that. But, in return, I'll expect you to verify the facts if you're questioned." As he spoke, he relented further. "I do owe you thanks for confessing this to me. It's one hell of a relief, as you can imagine."

"Glad to see your feelings change," Hawkins said, his own relief apparent.

Without another word, he turned and left.

Holt sat for a moment, thinking. Then he reached for a pencil and paper. Presently, he wrote out a few paragraphs describing what Hawkins had told him.

He got up then and took it into the press room and handed it to Gloria without a word.

She had just finished locking the type in the form, and was placing a news sheet of paper in the tympan, prior to pressing out a proof.

He gave her time to read the copy, then said, "Work this in somehow in the front page, Gloria. I want it read by every subscriber without delay. Can you imagine that heel Sam Braddock pulling off a stunt like this?"

She seemed shocked at first, unable to speak, and he knew then that the suspense of these past days also had taken a toll of her.

Unexpectedly then, she burst into tears. "Damn, damn, damn him!" she said.

"A lot of agonizing for nothing," he said.

He didn't know what else to say; in all the time he'd known her, he'd never before seen her cry.

Then as suddenly as they had begun, her tears stopped flowing.

That startled him into speaking. "Every day I kept looking at you, and you didn't appear concerned. You showed nothing."

"I suffered as you did," she said. "I'd have thought you'd know that."

"You should have told me."

"Why?"

"So I'd know you cared, dammit!"

"Of course, I cared!" she said.

"I can't read your mind."

"Some things are better left unsaid."

"Yes," he said. "But this wasn't one of them."

By noon the next day, the word was out that Sam Braddock had played a trick on the town in an attempt to aggravate Holt.

Of all the people irked by Braddock's hoax, none were more so than the saloon patrons who had been placing bets with McCleod.

McCleod himself was as angry as the rest of them, as he saw his expected commission on holding the bets slipping away.

He let go at Braddock, one of the few people who had not yet heard of the exposé of his fraud, the instant he came unsuspectingly through the doors of his place.

"There he is, men!" McCleod said. "The man who made damn fools of all of us! And put Bret Holt in a sweat, out of pure meanness."

Somebody, drunker than the rest, said, "Anybody got a rope?"

"What the hell are you talking about?" Braddock said.

McCleod told him, delivering his words as if they were bullets spewing from a six-gun.

"I intended it as a joke," Braddock said lamely.

"Some joke!" the one who'd asked about the rope said.

Braddock looked scared. He could tell this bunch had been drinking long before he'd got there. And a likkered-up crowd, he knew, was unpredictable. The man who planted the rope idea, might have been, more or less, kidding. But give a drinking bunch an idea like that and God knew what might come of it.

"Maybe it did get out of hand," Braddock said. "I can see now that I shouldn't have done it. All I can do now is ask you all to have a drink on me, and accept my apology."

The rope man changed his attitude at the offer of the free drink. "Me." He said quickly, "I accept. Set mine up, McCleod."

Still peeved, McCleod said, "Not unless the acceptance is unanimous."

The drunk said, "Dammit! that ain't fair, McCleod. Besides, we can't hang the town's only undertaker. All them corpses Wild Will Savage has been leaving around would stink up the place."

"I ain't talking about hanging," McCleod said. "I'm talking about, do all of you accept Sam's apology?"

Johnny Reno was on the edge of the crowd, and now he spoke in a loud, clear voice. "I don't." There was a cold anger in his words.

"Naturally, we'll call off our bet, Reno. Under the circumstances," Braddock said.

Reno studied him without speaking. His fingers went to the butt of his six-gun and he fondled it, thoughtfully.

"Well?" Braddock said nervously.

"No," Reno said. "It isn't off. I'm a gambler, Braddock. And I can usually spot a bluff when it's tried on me. I sensed something wrong when you insisted on that deadline on our bet."

"What are you getting at?"

"You know. Since you knew it was all a rumor about Canton being on his way, you figured to take no risk betting on Savage, while making yourself look big in the eyes of the town. You're a tinhorn, Braddock."

"Call me what you like, the bet is off, I say."

Reno' fingers gripped the handle of his gun. "I say no. You made the terms, and by God, you'll stick to them!" He turned to McCleod. "Right? You wrote down the deadline."

McCleod's dislike of Reno showed on his face, but he said, "Sam, he's right. You made the conditions, and you're stuck with them, for what little they're worth, until Tuesday afternoon at five o'clock."

CHAPTER 16

THE old man rode into Rosario on a dun gelding that looked to be as old as he was.

Bret Holt, standing outside his office in the bright morning sunshine, getting a breath of fresh air, watched him approach from the south. Holt's curiosity rose as the rider drew near.

The old man sat slouched in his saddle, and his trail-dusted range clothes were worn, but not yet patched. On his hip, belted high, was a holstered gun, and in a saddle boot was a rifle.

As he came abreast of Holt he reined up and gave a glance at the *Rosario Record* sign. He sat then, appraising Holt with faded gray eyes that matched the duck-billed hair shocking beneath the rear brim of his battered Stetson.

"I reckon maybe you're him," the old man said.

"Maybe," Bret said. "Maybe not."

"Name's Kid Sheehan," the old man said.

"No it isn't," Bret said. "I'm Holt. Bret Holt."

"Dammit, not you," the old man said. "*I'm* Kid Sheehan."

Holt pondered that, then said, "The name has a faintly familiar ring."

"That's the trouble, goddammit! Was a time it wasn't all that faint."

"Sheehan, Sheehan," Holt said.

"See what I mean?"

"Kit Sheehan," Holt said, racking his memory aloud.

"Not *Kit. Kid!*"

"Kid Sheehan!" Holt said. "I remember you. Scouted for

Kit Carson when he went into the Canyon de Chelly after the Navajos."

"That and a hell of a lot more you likely never heard about."

"I only read about the raid much later. I was off fighting in the big war about that time."

"I had a big name once," Sheehan said, "as a bounty hunter."

"You wanted to see me?"

"I heard there was a cantankerous bastard named Rufe Canton made a threat against you."

"So?"

"You want I should take him off your hands?"

Holt's jaw dropped. "You think you're a match for him?"

"I don't aim to pistol duel him," the old man said. He reached down his hand to slap his rifle stock. "I figured on more like an ambush."

"And the price?"

"What I need is a job for my old age. A nice cushy job somewheres as a marshal, maybe. A place like this would be fine."

"We've got a marshal," Holt said.

"So I heard. That's what brung me. I read about this young feller you call Wild Will Savage."

"Surely you didn't come to Rosario to call *him* out!"

"Hell, no! Not after reading a couple of them stories you writ about him. It's because of those stories that I'm offering to hunt down Canton and bushwhack him for you."

"In return for what?"

"For writing me up in one of them books like you done for Savage. It'd get my name back in front of folks again. Then, by God, they'd sit up and listen when I asked for a lawman job."

"You ever wear a star?"

"Nope. But I done my share of bounty-hunting over the

years. But sleeping out on the trail don't agree with me no more. Which is why I'm looking for a town job."

"For that, you'd hire out to do murder?"

"Killing is killing, ain't it? Bushwhacking was the easy way when a bounty said dead or alive."

"You're that desperate?"

"Way I see it, a chore like killing beats swamping out a saloon," Sheehan said. "And at my age, I can't be choosy." He paused. "And ain't you desperate, your own self?"

"Not that desperate," Bret said. "Not desperate enough to hire somebody to commit murder."

"You're young yet, with a good life ahead of you, except for Canton. I ain't."

"How old are you, Kid?"

"Old enough to be your father," Sheehan said. "But only if you had a whore for a mama."

"Considering your age, I'll let that comment pass."

"Hell, I didn't mean no offense. I was just stating a fact to the best of my knowledge," the Kid said. "So what about my proposition?"

"I told you no."

The old man said, fretfully, "I don't see what you got to lose."

"It goes against my conscience," Bret said. "That's reason enough."

"Your damn conscience can right well put you in a pine box."

"I guess I can't argue that point," Holt said. "But that's the way it is."

"No deal?"

"No deal, Kid."

Disapppointment showed on the Kid's grizzled face. Then he said, "How about writing me up, anyhow? I got plenty of stories to tell, you could put them in a book. We could split the profits, me taking a real small cut. All I'd need is a little grubstake to keep me eating."

Holt shook his head. "Sorry. I haven't been able to write lately, anyway. This Canton thing is too much on my mind."

"Ain't I just offered to fix that for you?"

Holt just stared at him, tired of discussing it.

After a considerable silence, Sheehan said, "Well hell. I got to eat. You happen to have a spare half-dollar on you?"

Holt fished a silver dollar from his pocket. He held it up for the old man to see, then tossed it to him.

"Obliged," the Kid said, catching it and clutching it tightly in his hand. "I see only one saloon up the street. They got a regular swamper to clean out the place?"

"Not now," Bret said. "Used to be Will Savage. But now he's the marshal."

The old man shook his head. "Beats all, don't it, how a man's life works out? Savage starts out a swamper, ends up famous and a marshal. I start out with an early reputation, and end up asking for a job cleaning out spittoons."

"Nobody said it was fair," Holt said.

The old man kicked the dun's flanks and moved off toward the saloon.

"Saloonkeeper's name is Jason McCleod," Holt called after him.

Sheehan kept on moving. Holt wondered if the Kid was hard of hearing.

Gloria's voice from the open doorway startled him.

"I heard the discussion, Bret," she said.

"By God, you've got to be quite the eavesdropper," he said, his voice rising. "And I don't like that."

She ignored his tone. "You should have taken him up on his offer."

"If you heard our talk, you know why I couldn't." He paused. "Besides, an old man like that, how could he kill Canton?"

"From ambush? It was a chance. Didn't he say he'd been a bounty hunter?"

"He did. And I'm beginning to recall that at one time he was. Bits and pieces come to mind of things I've heard about him. He goes way back. Scouted for the army long before the war. He's got to be way past sixty now." Holt paused. "He could be a source for a novel, at that."

"Be realistic, Bret. I'm not thinking about him as story material. I'm thinking of how to stop Rufe Canton."

"I will not hire an assassin."

"Noble Bret Holt!" she said angrily.

"Not noble," he said. "But I draw the line at bushwhacking."

"Didn't you see this could be a way to save Will from facing Rufe?"

"I saw," he said. "But even so—"

"You see nothing!" she cried. She turned away from him and disappeared within.

He followed her into the pressroom. "Why do we always fight?" he said.

"Because you are such a fool, sometimes. Like now."

"Do you believe the end justifies the means?" he said.

"If it means the end of Rufe Canton, I do!" Then her voice abruptly lost most of its rancor. "Oh, Bret," she said, "I don't want to argue with you. But can't you be practical? Must you always live by your feelings, instead of your head?"

He shrugged. "I've lived considerable time this way."

"And you may die this way, too," she said.

"I have my code."

"You *had* your code," she said. "And look where it got you."

"A man has to set a limit somewhere," he said. "A limit beyond which he will not go."

"*Some* men. The ones who are fools."

"Most men, I think."

"Women are not so foolish," she said.

"No? What do you call your insane obsession with vengeance?"

"There is nothing foolish about *that*," she said firmly. "Any woman would feel as I do."

He shook his head slowly, but said nothing.

"It's plain you do not want to understand,"

"It is more like I can't."

"Forget that part, then. I'm thinking of your survival," she said.

"I appreciate your concern. Lately, I've had the feeling that you no longer cared."

"I care."

"I mean the way I thought you once did."

"And what way was that, Bret?"

"Do you have to ask?"

"No," she said. "I guess not. I don't really know why my feeling has changed. But I do care, Bret."

"But in a different way, isn't that it?"

"Yes," she said, "that's it." She paused, meeting his eyes. "I'm sorry, Bret."

CHAPTER 17

THE old man hitched the dun to the tie rail in front of McCleod's place. Sheehan dismounted in sections, and ended up with his rundown right boot in the dust of Main street, and the toe of his left still in the stirrup.

McCleod, who had just opened the front doors, stood there watching. A couple of minutes passed, and he, thinking the old man was stuck in that position, started to move out to help him.

At that moment the old man, still clinging to the saddle horn with his left hand, reached with his right to grasp his stuck foot and work it loose. Freed, the foot slammed down hard enough to kick up a spurt of dust.

The old man turned then and saw McCleod staring at him. "Going to have to lengthen that stirrup some, I reckon," he said.

"If you do that," McCleod said, "your leg won't be long enough to reach it when you're in the saddle."

The old man thought about that. "Reckon that's why I ain't done it before," he said. "You open for business?"

"Just am," McCleod said.

"Free lunch set out yet?"

"Just did," McCleod said.

"Reckon I'll take a shot of rye whiskey, then."

"I sell it."

"I got money."

"Come on in," McCleod said.

The old man trailed him into the saloon, tripping once on the porch step.

At the bar, McCleod shoved out a glass and poured from a bottle.

The old man lifted the drink and tasted it. "God!" he said. "That's awful!"

"Don't drink it then."

"Well, it ain't that bad," he said, and downed it fast. "Name of Kid Sheehan," he said then.

McCleod gave him a closer look. "You're kidding!"

"Nope."

"Cripes, Kid, I served you years ago!" McCleod said. "But where, exactly, I don't rightly remember."

"Ten, twelve years back," Sheehan said, suddenly placing McCleod's face. "1871, in Abilene. You was working as a bartender in The Alamo."

"You've got a hell of a good memory."

"For those days I have," Sheehan said. "Can't say much for it lately."

McCleod refilled the glass. "What brings you to Rosario, Kid?"

"Like I told that writing feller down the street, I'm looking for a job."

"A job? What kind, Kid?"

"I wanted to do that feller Holt a favor, so's he'd write me up. Figured then I could get me a job law dogging."

"What favor?"

"Kill Rufe Canton."

"Big order."

"I ain't afraid of big orders, and never was."

"I recall," McCleod said.

"He turned me down," Sheehan said. "Peculiar cuss. Won't hire bushwhacking done."

"Sounds like Bret," McCleod said. "What now, then Kid?"

"I got to eat. And the bounty-hunting business has gone to hell for me, what with a lot of young punks coming in." Sheehan paused. "I heard maybe you could use a full-time swamper."

McCleod studied him thoughtfully. "Might be I could," he said.

"I'd need a place to sleep," the Kid said. "Sleeping under the stars makes my bones ache, anymore. You got a shed out back, maybe?"

McCleod was still thinking about it. At one time the old man did have something of a reputation. Having Kid Sheehan sweeping out the place just might be an added customer draw.

He said, "Might make a place for you in a storeroom."

"Be obliged," the old man said. "I'm still hoping to work some more on that writing feller, bring him around to trading favors."

"I wouldn't count on it," McCleod said.

"Maybe so," the Kid said. "But a man that puts in his years bounty hunting and bushwhacking learns to think positive."

"Kid," McCleod said, "you are a character."

"That's what I been trying to tell that writing feller," Sheehan said.

CHAPTER 18

THE town reverted now to a somnolent routine of living, though for a day or so after the revelation of Braddock's machinations, he was the target of considerable verbal abuse.

Even after the most heated resentment cooled down there was a lingering anger among those who had been aroused to active betting. Sam Braddock had become an unpopular man in Rosario.

Those with a gambling bent could forgive his lack of ethics. What they couldn't forgive was his causing them to reach a feverish high, only to have their anticipation dashed without their achieving satisfaction.

Even his standing for drinks at McCleod's bar was slow to lessen the ill-feeling against him.

Of course, being an undertaker, he was accustomed to a certain amount of mild ostracism among the citizenry, which was one reason he had made his showy bet on the now-popular figure, Marshal Savage. The bet that Johnny Reno was insisting on holding him to until the expiration of Braddock's own self-imposed deadline.

When all this started Braddock had hoped to become more popular himself. It sure as hell hadn't worked out that way.

Johnny Reno added to Braddock's discomfiture. It was as if he knew something that Braddock did not.

Every time he was around and Braddock looked at him, he found Reno staring. Like a cat looking at a caged bird, Braddock thought. It got on his nerves.

Finally, as they stood at McCleod' bar, only a patron or two apart, and Braddock felt Reno's stare upon him and turned to meet it, he could stand it no longer.

"What're you staring at all the time?" he said.

"I like to see a tinhorn taken," Reno said. His voice was cold.

Braddock backed down, clamping his mouth shut. Reno was still an unknown quantity in Rosario. He wore his gun as if he was familiar with its use. Being an undertaker, Braddock had seen a lot of dead men. He had no desire to become one.

But, after a brief silence, he was driven to speak again, this time without belligerency. "I know now, Reno, that I acted like a damn fool, starting that rumor. And, believe me, I'm sorry about it."

In that same cold voice, Reno said, "You may be even sorrier."

"What do you mean?"

For an answer, Reno turned to a stranger standing on his far side. "Tell Braddock here, what you told me a few minutes ago, outside there when you rode up," he said.

The stranger had a look about him as if he'd maybe tried to make a living on either side of the law. He showed a lot of hard use.

"Just rode in from old Fort Sumner," the stranger said. "I knowed Reno here from over Arizona way."

"Tell him about Canton," Reno said.

"Canton?" Braddock said.

"Yeah, Rufe Canton," the stranger said. "I mentioned to Reno that I'd sat in a poker game with Rufe, a couple of days back."

"Canton is at the old fort?"

"Was when I left. Had been there a couple of weeks. Said he was leaving the next day or so hisself. Said he was heading here to Rosario to take care of some unfinished business."

Braddock stood as if stunned. He didn't want to believe what he was hearing. Desperately, he cast about for flaws in the story. "Seems like if you were both coming a day apart, you'd have waited a day and travelled together," he said.

"I've played cards with Rufe a time or two," the man said, "Because he's a lousy poker player." He paused. "But I never ride with him. The son of a bitch is crazy. I'd be scared to sleep on the trail near him."

"He say what his unfinished business was?"

"Nope. And I never asked. But whatever it is, you can expect him to come riding in no more than a day and a half from now. Riding that big, black gelding of his."

Braddock took his eyes off the stranger and looked at Reno.

Reno, who had been coldly staring, suddenly broke into a grin. "All right, tinhorn," he said. "You tried to play a dirty trick on that editor you don't like. Now, you better go tell him that Canton is coming for real this time. It'll give him time to get his bodyguard ready. And you'd better make him believe you. That's if you have any hope of saving the five hundred you put on Savage."

"He won't believe me!"

"Maybe Savage will."

"He won't either. Not unless Holt does."

Reno nodded. "That's the way I see it, too. And it makes me feel real good."

"A day and a half?" Braddock said to the stranger.

"Maybe less," the stranger said. He paused, then said, "Me, I was heading for Socorro. But now that I know what Rufe meant by unfinished business, I think I'll stick around to see the fun."

"Some fun!" Braddock said.

Reno's grin grew wider. He said to the stranger, "Sam, here, laid his money on our part-time marshal, and now he's in a sweat." He explained how this had come about.

The stranger shook his head. "I've seen Rufe kill two men after calling them out," he said to Braddock. "And I wouldn't want to be holding your bet."

"Neither does Sam," Reno said.

Braddock gritted his teeth. Reno's jibe only made him feel

worse. If only he could find a way to delay Canton until after the deadline! he was thinking.

He didn't care what happened to Will Savage, really. And much less to Bret Holt. But he did hate to lose five hundred dollars to that miserable bastard Reno. And all because of a deadline that he, himself, had insisted on setting.

Braddock left the saloon, heading back to his drugstore. As he crossed Main, he caught sight of a rider coming up the street.

Reaching the portico of his shop, he turned for a second glance, and something about the rider's appearance caused him to wait.

Seeing this, the rider drew abreast and halted.

He was very young, wore a low-slung gun at his thigh. There was a rifle scabbard under his saddle fender, but it was empty of a weapon.

There was a kind of forlorn toughness to the cast of his face, and his worn-out saddle tramp clothes added to the aura of desperation.

"What you staring at, mister?" the youngster said.

"Sorry," Braddock said. "Didn't mean to." The kid looked desperate enough to be scary. Braddock turned toward the door of his place.

"Hold on!" the kid said. "I'm looking for a jasper called Savage. Where can I find him?"

"Up the street to the edge of Mex town. His office is alongside an old *calabozo*. It's our jail now."

"I heard he's got a big, big reputation now, ain't he?"

"Big enough." Braddock had him sized up as another bravo, looking for fame of his own. Like that kid Frank Hatch that he'd buried recently.

"He as good as they say he is?" the bravo said. "With a gun, I mean."

"Better," Braddock said. Even though he was an undertaker, he didn't enjoy burying kids.

"The better he is, the more famous the man who downs him," the stranger said. "Ain't that right?"

"Don't even think about it, son," Braddock said. "Seven men have tangled with him, the last few weeks. They're dead and he's still walking."

The kid shook his head. "Worth a try, anyhow. You know how it is to be a nothing?"

Braddock didn't, but he did not answer. His mind began to work on the kid's possibilities.

He said, "Like I said, you want to tangle with a lawman. You go against him, there's no way you can claim self-defense, even if you're lucky. You can't win with a deck like that. You either die or you kill him. If you kill him, you could be on the dodger list of every lawman in the Territory."

"Suits me," the youngster said. "My rep will grow then in a hurry. Better than being a nothing. Hell, man, I'm broke."

Braddock, studying the look of him, could believe that.

And although the youngster *might* kill Savage, in which case all bets, including his own with Reno, would be off, Braddock didn't think it likely.

He made a decision. "If you're needing money," he said, "forget Savage, for now. How'd you like to make forty dollars for killing a horse?"

"You joking?"

"Let me tell you what I mean," Braddock said.

CHAPTER 19

HOLT knew now that he should have run.

He sat tensely in his office.

A handful of citizens had volunteered at Jason McCleod's call for a committee to inform him that Canton was on his way, and that this time it was for real.

There were four of them standing before him now, part of the town council: Judd, Turner, Kelly and Hawkins. Only McCleod and Braddock were missing.

Holt's glance swept from one to another of them.

The strain of the job they'd come to do showed on their faces.

Holt gave George Hawkins a particular scrutiny. He had always assumed it was George who had joined Braddock in voting against his proposal to hire Will as marshal.

But now, Hawkins' expression had the same haunted look as the others. Even so, Holt was driven to touch on George's earlier role in Braddock's hoax.

He said, "I'm kind of surprised to see you here, bringing the warning, George." He paused. "Almost as surprised as if Sam had joined you."

Hawkins looked offended. "I told you how it was," he said.

"I suppose Sam is enjoying this," Holt said.

"I don't think so," Hawkins said, his voice rising. "As a matter of fact, he has bet against Canton."

Holt feigned surprise. "On me?"

"Well, no. But on Will."

"Well, that's downright encouraging," Holt said. "Who did he bet with?"

"Reno."

"And that's *dis*couraging, since Reno's profession is trying to pick winners."

Something in Holt's tone irked Hawkins. "You hadn't heard?"

"Well, I heard a rumor to that effect, George. But I've learned to be skeptical about rumors lately. You know?"

Hawkins glowered briefly, but almost at once his expression returned to its original concern. "I suppose so," he said.

It left Holt feeling sorry he'd badgered the man. His only excuse to himself was the stress he was under.

Kelly said, "Bret, all that ammunition you paid for on Will's account—I hope it pays off."

"And getting us to appoint him marshal," Judd said. "We're all hoping that pays off, too."

"As am I, gentlemen," Holt said.

Henry Turner, the mercantile owner, was eyeing him with curiosity. "I keep wondering how you feel, letting Marshal Savage step out to protect you in a personal quarrel."

"He's the law, isn't he?"

"You made him the law," Turner said.

"We *all* made him the law," Holt said. He said it a little too strongly, the words sounding false in his own ears.

He expected to hear one of them argue about it, but nobody did.

They're all feeling too sorry for me at this point, he thought. He hated knowing that.

He said, "Gentlemen, I thank you for bringing the word of what I have to expect."

"It isn't an easy thing to do, Bret," Judd said.

"I understand."

He understood, all right. The months of waiting were almost over.

A day, or a day and a half at the most, Judd had just told him. "That's what the stranger from Fort Sumner said."

"Maybe he was just talking," Holt said.

Judd shook his head. "He's known to Johnny Reno, and Reno says he's not that kind."

"Can we believe what Reno says?"

"You're grabbing at straws," Henry Turner said. "Why in hell don't you run, Bret?"

Holt was silent, then he said, "How?"

"Take the stage out."

"This is Monday. The stage won't come through on its run until Thursday," Holt said.

"I can see you've maybe given it thought," Mike Kelly said. "Trouble is, you've waited too long."

Walt Judd said, "I'll sell you a horse and saddle. You could leave now and maybe have a full day's lead."

"Even with a day's lead," Holt said, "what good would it do me? I haven't ridden in years."

"A rig, then?"

"How far would I get, with a trailwise pursuer like Canton on my tail?"

Nobody answered.

"Like I said," Kelly said, "you waited too long. All these months you waited, and now it's too late."

Judd said now, "I reckon Will Savage will be stopping by, shortly. Jason told us to let him know first."

"Where'd you find him?" Holt said tonelessly.

"The Widow Lavender's, where else?"

To Holt, all this had an aura of *deja vu.*

He had known, of course, that the time would come. But the reprieve from his earlier expectancy had strangely enough given him a false sense of security.

Now he swore at himself for being so foolish.

Turner suddenly said, "About that thirty dollars on your merchandise account, Bret—forget it."

Holt looked up and stared at him, silent.

Turner fidgeted under the stare. After a moment, he said, "It's been bothering me that I asked for it that other time."

When Holt still did not speak, Turner said to the others,

"Let's get back to McCleod's. We've done our chore here. And, who knows, Canton might be riding in any time. It's damn sure he'll stop at Jason's first off."

They all began to file out. None of them spoke. None of them could think of anything appropriate to say.

CHAPTER 20

WILL had left the arms of the widow to take the message of the councilmen sent by Jason McCleod.

When they had gone, he returned only briefly to her, felt her tears, used his strength to free himself from her embrace.

"I've got to go," he said. "The time is near."

She did not ask if he would return.

It was not her way to question him. And he was grateful for that because, of course, he did not know the answer.

He knew that long ago she had lost a husband she loved. Now she took what solace from Will as he could give, and asked nothing more of him.

Just as he had taken his solace from her, after many young years of doing without.

So now, as he left her place, he said only to her, "Goodbye."

And she made no reply. He imagined she was thinking back to her earlier loss.

He had seen tears in her eyes when he left. Was she mourning me, as she had mourned her husband, he wondered. Does she *know*?

With the thought, all the months of his burgeoning confidence began to crumble, despite his efforts to stop it.

All that growth—from being Will, saddle tramp and handyman, to becoming Wild Will Savage, *Man of the West*—deserted him. Washed away by the Widow's tears.

He had been riding high on his growing prestige. It had sustained him. But now, suddenly, that sustenance was gone.

It had come too fast, he thought. It had come too easy.

Easy come, easy go, he thought, and was angry at the thinking of it.

Before this time in Rosario, before this time that began when Bret Holt picked him as the protagonist for his novels, nothing had ever come easy for Will.

It wasn't that he was stupid, he knew. It was more that he was a slow learner, or a difficult learner, and there always seemed to be a limit to any proficiency he eventually acquired.

He was aware that he had never in his life reached more than a level of mediocrity in any pursuit he had tried. He had been a mediocre cowhand, hardworking but the first to be laid off in the slack seasons.

And this after growing up on a bachelor uncle's ranch from the age of twelve, following the massacre of his parents and sister during a renegade Indian raid on their meager Kansas homestead.

At eighteen he'd left the uncle, a not unkindly man who could not hide his increasing irritation at his ward's limitations, and did not argue against Will's going.

Things had never got better for Will.

Not until Bret Holt had become his patron, of sorts. This had led to his unexpected proficiency with a six-gun, a talent he might never have discovered otherwise.

And it had led to his first experience with pride.

A pride that had lasted until now.

Now, when he needed it most. When it was washed away by a woman's tears. Tears of mourning that meant she believed he was about to die.

And for that he hated her, and cursed her silently for robbing him of what he most needed as he prepared to go out to face Rufe Canton.

Cursed her in spite of all the solace she had given him through the months. Cursed her despite the gratefulness he felt toward her, and would always feel, until the day he died.

A chill took his spine as he thought of that.

The day he died.

Would it be today? Tomorrow?

Did she *know*?

Women had intuitions that men did not have. He knew that, although he had not known many women. He believed that strongly enough that her tears, warm as they were, chilled him.

Fear wracked him as it never had.

All the years that he had achieved little had given him a sense of being impervious to disaster—never attaining much, he had little to lose.

Now, having acquired fame, he found himself facing the loss of it, and the loss of his life. His fears had never been tempered by the lesser crises experienced by ambitious men.

He stood outside the front door of her house and thought for a moment of returning to her. But instead, he stepped out onto the street.

And, at once, he found himself throwing back his shoulders, standing tall, and taking his steps with the faint swagger he had acquired as part of his public image.

Briefly, he felt better.

And he realized that was because he had stepped into the boots of Wild Will Savage, Marshal. He was playing a part when he swaggered, as an actor played a part when he made an entrance onto a theater stage.

He had put himself into the role written for him by Holt.

Man of the West was only fiction, about a character who sprang from Holt's imagination. Wild Will Savage isn't me, Will thought, so I have nothing to fear.

He felt himself swaggering more than the role called for, and adjusted a little to correct it.

Thus walking, he approached the office of the *Record* where he would remain with Holt until the show was over, he thought.

Until Rufe Canton came walking down the street.

But would Canton understand it was all a theatrical?

He would not, he thought. And his fear came back.

No one was in the office. Will went to the shop door and saw Gloria entering from the rear door, and judged she was returning from the privy.

He did not hail her; at the moment he had no desire to talk with her. Instead, he seated himself in the chair behind Holt's desk.

Almost at once his eyes fell on the pages of the novel manuscript that Holt had apparently been working on.

He lifted a sheet and began to read:

The day approached, that dreaded day when Rufe Canton was to return . . .

He paused and thought about that. Did Holt know today was the day? He began to read again, then impatiently started skipping through, wanting to know the ending.

And now Rufe Canton stepped out onto the main street and began his walk toward where Wild Will Savage fearlessly awaited him . . .

Fearlessly? Will felt the chill again and read on.

Wild Will, seeing Canton through the Record's window, went to the door and exited to meet him.

With measured steps they began pacing the half-block of distance between them.

Even from afar, Will could see the wolfish grin that bared Canton's teeth. Canton was enjoying this. This was what he lived for.

Will moved forward, unafraid. But his handsome face was somber. Killing was not something that gave him pleasure. Killing was what he did when there was no other way. Killing was what he would do now, because Canton gave him no choice.

Now, at last, he, Will Savage, would know who was the best.

From far back in his childhood, before his mother had died, he recalled suddenly her reading to him from a book about King Arthur's court in the early, chivalrous days of old England.

A phrase came to his mind, a phrase spoken by that Knight of the Round Table, most noble of them all, Sir Galahad: "My strength is of the strength of ten, because my heart is pure."

The phrase jolted Will. Three things were wrong there: One, Will had no remembrance of his mother ever reading to him. Two, how much use was strength, when you were using six-guns? And, three, the whole thing made him seem like a nance.

Then his eyes caught the next action as he and Canton made simultaneous draws:

Wild Will, having knocked down the cold-blooded killer with his first shot, calmly emptied his gun into Canton as he lay begging for mercy.

Emptied his gun as Canton had once done into Will's friend. Only, now, Savage saved a last bullet for the coup de grace. The Man of the West thus made sure the psychopathic gunman would kill no more.

As he read the ending, Will felt the cold fear leave him. This is how it can be, he thought. *This is how it will be.*

And he felt his self-confidence return.

CHAPTER 21

BRET Holt had been driven to write that ending.

Driven by the guilt that haunted him through the long period of his succumbing to Gloria's plotting to use Will.

But even as he resolved Will's fate with a happy ending on the manuscript pages, his doubts overwhelmed his hope that it would occur that way.

How could it?

Deep down he knew he had created a newsprint hero. A gunman who shot paper bullets.

The saga of Wild Will Savage was built of exaggerated freak accidents and lucky coincidences, colored by Holt's own hand, for the most part.

True, Will had gained considerable skill with a gun. But who, really, had he ever faced that approached the deadly caliber of Rufe Canton?

Chango Carmona?

Carmona would have easily killed Will if he hadn't been so drunk he'd forgot he emptied his gun in a shooting gallery.

Young Frank Hatch?

An inept eighteen-year-old kid, trying to emulate a famous father.

The Buck Hollister bunch?

A band of rustlers turned bumbling would-be bank robbers.

Solo Gurk?

Taken by surprise, under ridiculous circumstances.

The Deppler posse?

Out-bluffed by Will, aided by its mutinous members.

Running over this list mentally, Holt knew Will had no real chance.

He, Holt, had been deceiving himself, had come to believe his own written hyperbole because he wanted to believe it. Because he had come to *have* to believe it.

It had become the only hope he had.

And, now, he clearly saw the deception, and was terrified by what remained: there was no hope. No hope for Will Savage, and, by extension, there was no hope for Bret Holt.

All he had achieved was the placing of poor Will as first target.

And, for that, he was overwhelmed by guilt.

Why had he involved Will? It was none of Will's affair.

Once he had told Will that, that other time when Canton came walking down the street. He had insisted then that Will stay out of it.

But after Holt lost his courage, he had succumbed to involving poor Will.

He cursed himself. What had this scheme gained him except guilt to add to the burden of his fear?

There's no hope for me, he thought. But there could be for Will if Holt could keep him out of this.

Canton would not hunt down Will. He had said he would return to shoot Holt. He had not mentioned Will.

The fact that Will had been made town marshal shouldn't change Canton's object.

Not if Will stayed hidden. Out of sight until it was all over—meaning until Holt lay once again in the street, shot up and bleeding. Or , if he's lucky, already dead.

That was the worst terror—not the dying, but the living in agony, with four or five lead slugs in his body.

And that was what Canton had promised. That was what Canton would do. Canton was a man who'd live up to his threats, insane though they might be.

The horror of his fate made Holt face the ignominious truth about himself: *I will let Will go out there and be first target.*

I have come to that. The once-brave, outspoken editor of the Rosario Record *has come to that.*

Once-brave. . . . Where did my courage go? Where did the courage go that kept me fighting through the bitter years of the War of the Rebellion?

The courage that kept me fighting later in editorials for what I believed was right, and against what I believed was wrong?

Where did it go? It went into the dirt of Main street, gushing from the bullet holes blasted by Canton.

The sun-baked, dry, thirsty dirt that is there waiting to drink my blood again.

Is it that once lost, courage can never be regained?

I have come to believe so. What courage I had has never returned, in all the long months I have waited for Canton's return.

Not even a trace of it.

Not even a hope of it.

CHAPTER 22

HOLT came into the office, and Will got up from his desk. "So it's getting close," Will said.

"We knew it would come, Will."

"Sure."

There was an uncomfortable silence between them broken finally by Holt. "I never thought I'd take refuge behind another man," he said.

"I understand," Will said. "And I remember that you didn't that other time." He paused. "That was lucky for me. I wouldn't have stood a chance then."

"And now?"

"I'm a match for him now," Savage said. "I've got this curiosity, too. It's been with me, day and night, lately. It's something I got to know."

Holt said, "You mean, who is best?"

"Yes."

"Gunfighter's syndrome," Holt said. "God help me, I feel responsible for that."

"I don't blame you. You gave me something to be proud of."

"You have grown with it," Holt said. "But I don't know if that was for the best."

"We'll soon know, won't we?"

"I can't be that casual about it," Holt said. "How can you be?"

Will shrugged. "It ain't that I take it light. But I got to know."

"God help the both of us, then," Holt said.

"Can I talk to Gloria a minute?"

"She's back there."

Will turned and walked into the pressroom.

Holt stood up and started to follow, then thought better of it. Let him have his time with her, he thought. What there was between them was no longer his concern. Let the warrior have his glory with her, if he could. How many times had such a woman's kiss sent a man forth to perform—or to die— heroically in battle?

She looked up from the press as Will approached. She was surprised to see him. He had not contacted her since that evening at her house.

"Did Mr. Holt tell you?" he said.

"Tell me what, Will?"

"Word is that Rufe is really coming."

"Word from who?"

"A rider from Fort Sumner. Friend of Reno's. Rufe told him he'd be reaching here today or tomorrow. For unfinished business."

"Oh, Will!"

"Wish me luck."

"Oh, God!" she said. "You know I do, Will!"

"You want me to shoot him in the heart, or gut-shoot him?"

There was a tinge of sarcasm there that she missed. "Don't take any chances," she said.

"Just make sure he's dead. That's what you want, ain't it?"

"More than you can believe," she said.

"You are a hard woman, Gloria," he said, thinking of how different her farewell was from the Widow's.

"Why do you say that?"

He shook his head. "Don't you know? If you don't, there's no use me saying it."

"Maybe I am hard," she said. "But only in this one thing. I can be soft, too, Will. I thought you knew that. I thought I let you know that time at my house." She reached out and touched his arm and began to softly knead it with her fingers. "After this is over, Will, there can be other times. We're both young, Will. Don't you feel that *something* between us?"

"Maybe."

"Maybe? That's all?" She frowned. Her voice rose. "Will, how old is that Lavender woman?"

"I don't know. I never asked her."

"She's older than us. Doesn't that make a difference?"

"Don't seem to," Will said.

"I can give you more than she can—ever."

He was silent.

"I'm so proud of you," she said.

"Why?"

"Going out to meet Canton."

"I'm the marshal" he said. "It's my job."

"I like to think you are doing it for me," she said. "And that I can reward you for it."

Again he was silent.

"You know what I'm saying, Will?"

"I reckon I do," he said.

"How does it make you feel?"

"To tell you the truth, it ought to fire me up more than it does."

"I'm disappointed."

"Could be because I just come from the Widow's place," Will said. Again, his sarcasm eluded her.

"Goddam her!" Gloria cried. "Always her!"

"I figured I ought to live it up these last few hours before the meeting."

"Forget her!" Gloria said. "You are going to win! And you come to me when it's over."

Will thought for a moment, then said, "Bret gave me a line to say in one of the stories he writ. '*to the victor belongs the spoils.*' Is that what you mean?"

She scowled. "It could be worded better." she said.

As the word spread of Rufe's certain soon arrival, the crowd flocked back to McCleod's place.

McCleod's spirits rose. Although he was annoyed that neither Savage nor Holt put in an appearance, he expected they would do so shortly. And men were arguing over the probable outcome of the nearing action even more excitedly than before, some were laying bets, and all were drinking heavily of his rotgut whiskey.

What else could he ask for, he told himself.

Even Braddock, unnerved as he had first been by the news, could not stay away.

McCleod was, in fact, a little curious about the apparent calm with which Braddock was now taking it. But he was too busy serving drinks to give much thought to it.

During a brief lull though, he happened to glance at the wall clock and was startled to see how quickly the afternoon was passing. It was already past three o'clock. And this was Tuesday, and he was reminded of Braddock's bet deadline.

Twenty miles out on the road from old Fort Sumner, the young bravo, hired by Braddock, had been lying low, hidden in the scrub. He had a good view of the road, but it was tiresome waiting.

To break the boredom, and to keep from dozing off, he from time to time confided to his horse, tethered nearby, his wonder about his hire.

"The man told me to wait out here at the pass. Less'n I see him sooner. He'll be riding a big, black horse, he said. Kill the horse, but don't shoot the rider. Just leave him stranded. For that I get forty dollars, half up front.

" 'Make it fifty, and I'll kill the man,' I told him. 'No, goddammit!' he said. 'if that man don't walk into Rosario a couple days from now, you don't get paid the other twenty. I will not murder a man to save five hundred dollars, but I will murder a horse.'

"Mighty peculiar doings, if you ask me," the young bravo said. Getting no comment from the horse, he relapsed into silence, as he continued his vigil.

In early afternoon, he saw a rider on a black horse approaching. He sighted in on the horse with the Winchester rifle that Braddock had loaned him, and fired.

As the afternoon passed, Braddock's concern lessened with each passing minute. He congratulated himself for sending that kid out to delay Canton.

Finally, as evening neared, he could restrain himself no longer. He said to McCleod, "You can tear up that betting slip between me and Reno. The deadline is past. The bet is off."

McCleod looked at the clock. "Not quite," he said. "There's still an hour yet."

"You going to quibble over minutes?"

"There's Reno over there. You want to argue with him? He could be handy with that gun he wears."

"Have it your way," Braddock said. McCleod was right. Why take a risk arguing with Reno this late in the game? He was almost home free, now.

"Pour me another drink," Braddock said. By God, I'll be glad when the time is up, he was thinking.

He turned then, drink in hand, and surveyed the crowded saloon, just as the batwing doors swung inward.

Rufe Canton stepped in. His eyes, by chance, met Braddock's. In a loud voice, to be heard over the crowd's din, he called, "I got a damn fool kid slung dead over his saddle outside. He took a shot at me and missed, back on the trail a ways."

Braddock paled, but called back in the silence that followed. "Bret Holt knew you were coming."

"Good," Canton said. He strode toward the bar, as the crowd made way for him. "He's the one I came all the way back to see."

Somebody said, "We got a marshal here now, Canton."

"A marshal!" Canton grinned. "Who?"

"Will Savage."

Canton burst out laughing. "Reckon I've heard everything now."

A half-drunk cowboy said, "Well, I got twenty here to put on Savage!" He looked a little scared after he said it.

"What the hell is he talking about?" Canton said.

McCleod answered. "The boys have been wagering some on you facing off Savage."

Canton scowled, and started toward the cowboy. He was stopped by an old man pushing a broom across his path, stirring up the dust. Canton came close to tripping over the extended handle.

"Dammit! old man," Canton said. "Watch what the hell you're doing!"

The old swamper appeared not to hear. Sheehan went right on pushing the broom, crossing in front of Canton, and moving on, seemingly intent on his sweeping.

Canton turned toward the bar and called out to McCleod, "What the hell's he sweeping now for?"

For answer, McCleod lifted his hand and tapped a forefinger against his temple.

Canton growled something under his breath, and started again for the half-drunk puncher.

The old man pivoted abruptly and reached far to thrust the broom in his way.

It brought Canton up short again. His face showed fury.

He jerked his gun from his holster, and brought it up in a swinging arc, the barrel slamming against the old man's temple.

The old man dropped as if he'd been shot. Blood began to run out of his ear.

Everybody stared at the old man lying there. Nobody spoke for a long moment.

Then Canton said, "McCleod, what do you hire a damn old fool like that for?"

"He needed a job," the saloon keeper said.

"So?"

"That's Kid Sheehan laying there."

"Who the hell is Kid Sheehan?" Canton said.

"In his day," McCleod said, "he brung in his share of border jumpers and the like."

"Lawman?" Canton said.

"Bounty hunter."

"Fell a long way, didn't he?"

"Happens when a man lives too long," McCleod said.

Canton looked down on the unconscious form of Sheehan.

"Crazy old coot," he said. "Couldn't even handle that broom rightly."

"It was new to him" McCleod said. "He was a damn sight better with a rifle."

"Friend of yours?"

"I knew him."

"You sound kind of hard-nosed about me clipping him. It bother you that much?"

"Not near as much as it will him," McCleod said. "If he ain't dead."

Canton bent down and slapped his hand back and forth against Sheehan's jowls. "Hey, old man, wake up! You got Jason worrying about you."

The old man stirred, then sat up. Blood was still coming out of his ear. They all watched as he got slowly to his feet.

He stood there, staring at Canton for awhile, then picked up the dropped broom and walked unsteadily toward the rear door of the saloon, and disappeared.

Johnny Reno was standing close to Canton, and now he said, "You shouldn't have hit the old man like that."

"You want to buy in?"

Reno was slow to answer, but he finally said, "No, I guess not." He paused. "But maybe he will."

"Old man like him, what can he do?"

Reno shrugged. "Who knows?" he said.

Canton looked in the crowd for the reckless cowboy, but he had disappeared. He called out then, "Who else besides that fool puncher would bet on a joker like Will Savage?"

Most eyes turned toward Sam Braddock.

"You?" Canton said.

Braddock started to explain how he'd bet but placed a deadline on Canton's arrival. Just in time he realized that could be disastrous. He broke off abruptly, then ended lamely. "It was a damn fool way to bet, I know that now."

Canton eyed him suspiciously. "You might end up burying yourself, as well as that dead kid I brought in. Somebody put him out there to bushwhack me."

Braddock's pallor grew. He'd just remembered that the rifle he loaned the kid was one he'd kept racked for years behind the counter in his drugstore. He hoped to hell Canton didn't somehow recognize it.

McCleod said, "Ain't too much Savage money around. What there is of it, is out of town bettors, like that cowboy you heard. And he got three to one odds."

"Interesting," Canton said. "But Holt is the one I came to see."

"Ain't no money on *him*, if that's what you mean. Not after what you did to him the last time."

"I kind of thought he'd leave the Territory."

McCleod shrugged. "He always was a stubborn cuss."

"He won't be for much longer," Canton said.

CHAPTER 23

JOHNNY Reno couldn't get the old man out of his mind.

Like Canton, he didn't recall ever hearing the old man's name before McCleod mentioned it. Kid Sheehan. Before my time, he thought.

Maybe it was seeing the old man clubbed down that way by Canton, that bothered him. For all his gambler's cool, Reno was not a brutal man.

That was one side of it. But there was the other side, too. The side that touched him where he lived, or, more exactly, touched where he made his living.

Here he was with a sure-thing bet, he judged, with his money on Canton, and with that weasely Sam Braddock in a sweat over the outcome, and he should have been riding a high.

Instead, the whole thing was soured by the incident of the old man being dropped by Canton's pistol barrel.

Bleeding from the ear. Somehow that enraged Reno. And the picture of the old man staggering away with his broom, that angered him further.

Canton was going to make him five hundred dollars richer, but he hated Canton because of what he'd done to Sheehan.

It made him almost willing to forfeit his own five hundred just to see Canton lose.

Almost, he thought cynically, but not quite.

As a gambler he had to think of the money first. As a gambler he shouldn't let his emotions affect his goal of winning.

It was a flaw of his, he knew, that on rare occasions he let this happen.

Bothered by the thought, he worked his way to the bar and ordered a drink and downed it.

Someone shouldered in beside him, and, even before he looked, he sensed it was Canton.

"Have one on me," Canton said.

Reno lifted his empty glass. "Thanks, no, I just had one."

Canton seemed to take no offense. He said, "I understand you're the one backing me against that fool Braddock's bet."

"So happens I am."

"Easy money for you," Canton said.

Reno was silent. Not as easy as you think, was his thought, as the picture of old Kid Sheehan lying on the saloon floor came back to him.

"But, hell," Canton said, "a gambler like you lives by picking winners. Right?"

Reno didn't answer. Instead, he said again, and knowing he was a damned fool for doing so, "You shouldn't have hit the old man like you did."

Canton's half-friendly manner left him. "Maybe you ain't as smart as I thought you was." He paused, then said, "You said that before. That old coot a friend of yours?"

"No."

"In that case, you ain't acting too intelligent. I asked a while ago, you want to buy in?"

Reno hesitated, temper rising in him.

"Well?"

Reno shook his head finally. "Like I said, he isn't a friend of mine."

"You keep saying what you did, I'm going to think he is," Rufe said.

Reno fought his temper down. "I don't guess I'll say it again."

"In that case, you'll have a drink with me," Canton said.

"Yeah," Reno said, the fire gone out of him. "I guess I will."

McCleod poured them drinks, as Canton signaled. Canton raised his and waited, cold eyes staring at Reno.

Reno lifted his quickly and tossed it down. He had no desire to savor it.

And, at that moment, the old man came staggering back into the saloon.

Reno caught sight of him first, and instinctively his eyes searched him for sight of a weapon.

But the old man was armed only with his broom. Blood still trickling out of his ear.

He began trying again to sweep the floor, but he was having trouble with his balance, and kept bumping into the drinkers and tables and chairs.

Canton, at the bar, raised his voice to McCleod, "Get that damn old coot out of here."

McCleod looked out on the floor and saw the old man stumbling around.

Canton gave a sudden chuckle. "Hell, the old bastard looks drunker than a hoot owl."

"I don't think so," Reno said. "I think he's hurt bad."

"You blaming me for that?" Canton said.

"Just stating a fact." A little heat crept back into Reno's voice, despite his effort to contain it.

McCleod called out, "Hey, Kid! Forget the sweeping."

The old man didn't seem to hear him.

"Can't hold his likker," Canton said, and chuckled again.

Reno held back a comment.

Jason went to the end of the bar and came around, and went over to Sheehan and put his arm across his shoulders. "Take the rest the afternoon off, Kid. Go lay down and rest, you hear me?"

"I got a headache bad," Sheehan said.

"So do what I tell you. Go lay down."

"Yeah," he said. "Maybe I'll do that."

He didn't move, though. He just stood there and began

staring around him at the different patrons who were watching him now.

His eyes fell on Canton, and he stopped moving his head.

"He's the one that done it," Sheehan said.

"Quiet, Kid," McCleod said. "You don't want any more damn trouble."

Canton heard McCleod, and said, "You don't know that. Maybe he does." He addressed Sheehan. "You want more trouble with me, *Kid Sheehan?*" He grinned as he emphasized the name.

Sheehan shrugged loose from McCleod and staggered over close to Canton. He stood there facing him, teetering unsteadily.

"You shouldn't made my head ache," he said.

"Well now, that's a matter of opinion," Canton said. "You were making me trouble with that broom of yours."

"Wasn't my intention," the Kid said. "I ain't too handy with a broom."

"Appears that way to me, too. Maybe you ought to stick to the tools you're used to." Canton paused. "McCleod said you're some better with a rifle. Leastwise that you were at one time. You and me, maybe we ought to have a contest."

The old man's eyes fastened on Canton's and wouldn't let go. He didn't say anything, just held the stare.

Canton stared back. At first he was grinning, but then the half-crazy look in the old man's eyes began to get to him.

He turned to McCleod. "The old bastard is loco, can't you see that? Get him the hell out of here before I crack the other side of his skull."

McCleod said, "Come on, Kid, back to your quarters. You'll feel better laying down."

"Geeschrize!" Canton said as McCleod led the Kid away. "What's McCleod doing, hiring a crazy old coot like that?"

"He knew him a long time back," Johnny Reno said.

"It must have been a hell of a long time, by the looks of him."

"Not as long, maybe, as you'd think," Reno said. "He led a hard life, and when a man like that reaches a certain age, it has a way of catching up with him."

"He keeps pushing his luck," Canton said, "he's going to get caught up by something else."

CHAPTER 24

IT was *deja vu*, all right.

That feeling lent an unreality to what was about to happen, Holt thought. This time, though, it was nearing sundown.

There he was in his office, and the two saloon patrons had just left, the same ones who had warned him that other time.

But this time Will Savage was with him, had been staying on the *Record* premises since the previous day.

Gloria was there, too, and had refused to leave.

At first he had argued. But she was adamant, insisting this was the day she had been waiting for.

When she told him that, anger took him, so that he thought: You blood-thirsty bitch! And said, "Stay then, if that's what you want, and be damned to you! You want a front-row seat, like this is a theatre spectacle? Take it!"

"I *have* to be here," she said.

Holt met the eyes of Will, who was standing beside her. There was nothing he could read there. Will seemed oblivious to their quarreling. Most likely, his mind was on what was coming.

Holt did not look at Gloria again. At that moment he wanted her out of his sight.

She seemed to know that, and slipped quietly into the pressroom.

"He'll be coming down that street in a few minutes," Holt said.

Will nodded. "Yeah."

"For God's sake, Will! Is that all you've got to say?"

"What should I say?" Will said. He had gone to the window

173

and was looking out. "When I see him coming, I'll step out to meet him."

"You've got guts, Will."

"I saw you do it once."

Holt said. "Yeah, once."

"I'm better than you were. With a gun, I mean."

"Yes, you are," Holt said. He wanted to ask, *But are you better than Canton?* But he didn't.

He joined Will, staring out of the window.

A man suddenly came out of the saloon and stood in the shadow of the portico, surveying the street.

Holt felt Will go tense. He said, "That's Johnny Reno, Will."

"Yeah," Will said. He sounded relieved. "What's he doing there?"

"Wants a good view of what'll take place, I guess."

"Goddam his eyes!" Will said.

Johnny Reno was using those eyes that Will was damning.

He was following up on a gambler's hunch that had been with him since earlier that afternoon.

He was scanning the street between where he stood and the *Record* office where he assumed Bret Holt, and most likely Will Savage, were waiting.

He kept studying the board front structures that lined each side of Main. Most adjoined, with here and there a narrow pass-way to allow squeezing access to the rear premises.

There was nothing there that he could see. In a way he was disappointed. In another way, he was relieved.

Behind him the saloon's batwing doors swung open and Rufe Canton came out, followed by a spew of patrons.

The patrons came over and bunched up beside Reno, who stood there on the porch, his frock coat pulled aside to bare his holstered gun, as Canton stepped down into the street.

One of the townsmen noticed his stance, stared, and then

said, "Hell, Reno, are you in on this?" He nodded toward the visible weapon.

Nobody seemed to hear him, as all eyes were now on Canton.

Canton looked first up to the north, giving that direction a cursory glance. Satisfied, he turned back and gave Reno a quick appraisal, then faced south and commenced his walk down the block.

It was a long walk, Reno thought.

And suddenly his hunch was back, stronger than ever.

He could pick the spot where it ought to happen—thirty yards this side of the newspaper office. There where a narrow passage between structures could hide a man with a grudge.

Too cocky for his own good, Reno thought, meaning Canton. Careless in his arrogance.

Reno's first impulse was to cry out a warning, in a cold-blooded gambler's instinct to save his five-hundred-dollar bet.

The cry died in his throat as his recalled the sight of Canton pistol-whipping the old man to the floor.

The dirty, rotten son of a bitch, Reno thought. He shouldn't have done that.

In Holt's office Will Savage stood behind the glass, unmoving.

Holt's Shopkeeper Colt was lying on top of the counter.

Holt stepped over and picked it up and stared at it.

Will still hadn't moved.

"Are you going out?" Holt said.

Will didn't answer.

Holt knew then. Will wasn't going out.

Will had lost *his* nerve.

The same as I lost mine, Holt thought. He could not blame Will for that.

Without thought of what he was doing, Holt shoved past Will and exited onto the street.

Canton halted, looked surprised, saw Holt's gun in his hand, and whipped out his own, bringing it up to aim.

And from the corner of his eye, he saw old Kid Sheehan on his right, stepping from between two buildings with a rifle held hip high.

In reflex, Canton twisted to put a bullet into the old man's belly. Sheehan was driven back, dropping his unfired weapon.

Holt, shocked by the action, fired hurriedly and missed, and Canton's next shot knocked him down.

Behind him he heard Will fire even as Canton did again, a fraction quicker. He heard Will's groan.

From the prone, Holt fired again. He saw his slug smash into Canton' chest, driving him back and down, to lie unmoving.

He heard Will's bootsteps approaching until he stood over Holt, breathing hard. He could feel the blood dripping on him from above, and knew that Will was wounded, too.

And he could feel the blood gushing from his own wound in his thigh. It was the last thing he felt for awhile.

Morning finally came, after a pain-filled and restless night. He was at Gloria's place, lying alone in her bed.

Once again, old Doc Sanderson was tending to him, checking the dressing he had placed the previous evening.

Gloria stood by, watching.

He said to Doc, "Is Will all right?"

"Another damn fool," Sanderson said. "But of course he's all right." He paused, then said, more softly, "I fixed up his shoulder and I left him in the Widow Lavender's good hands."

A moment later he was stomping to the door, leaving without another word.

Gloria came close then and reached to take Holt's hand.

She said, "Bret, I saw it all from the window. It was a brave thing you did, and I'm proud of you."

He was silent.

"It was your shot that killed Rufe, not Will's," she said.

"I know that."

"But it isn't what the town will believe," she said. "Because it isn't what they want to believe. To them, Will is the hero."

"Too bad for him."

"It's better this way," she said.

"No," he said. "More than ever now it will make him the target for every glory-hunting killer in the Territory."

"Better him than you, Bret."

"No," he said again. "It will be on my conscience the rest of my life."

"Look at it this way," she said. "You've given him a fame he could never have achieved on his own. He'll likely go down in the annals of the West. His name will be remembered generations from now."

"And if he dies because I gave him fame, will it be worth it?"

"Many a man would think so," she said.

"But *you* are *my* hero, Bret! It was you who got me my revenge."

She leaned over him and pressed her lips to his.

She was surprised when he did not respond.

If you have enjoyed this book and would like to receive details of other Walker Western titles, please write to:

Western Editor
Walker and Company
720 Fifth Avenue
New York, NY 10019